MANSFIELD LETTERS

MANSFIELD LETTERS

Paula Atchia

The Book Guild Ltd
Sussex, England

The Book Guild Ltd
25 High Street,
Lewes, Sussex

First published 1996
© Paula Atchia, 1996
Set in Bembo
Typesetting by Poole Typesetting (Wessex) Ltd
Bournemouth, Dorset.
Printed in Great Britain by
Bookcraft (Bath) Ltd, Avon

A catalogue record for this book is
available from the British Library

ISBN 1 85776 118 9

For Michael, with love

AUTHOR'S FOREWORD

If ever a book was written purely for the author's personal pleasure and satisfaction, this one was.

I planned it five years ago with two clear aims: firstly, to see whether I could sustain writing an entire (albeit rather short) novel in Jane Austen's style; and secondly, to attempt to reinstate the character of Henry Crawford from *Mansfield Park* – often deemed unjustly wronged by his creator at the end of the work.

With regard to the first and subservient aim, what started out as an amusing exercise soon became fastidious; the attempt would have been abandoned after three chapters were I not by then thoroughly engaged in the main task, and absorbed in the dynamic of the story. But I conscientiously and constantly revisited the vocabulary and grammar with a view to respecting Jane Austen's writing, and have knowingly used very few words which are not found in any of her works. In the same way, I tried to use incidents that existed already in one or other of her novels, and was careful in the introduction of new characters to remain within the same parameters, though I had to dig into memorabilia for Henry Crawford's return from India, and the brief sojourn of the thirsty nurse.

What is the use of such a task? Apparently none, I am afraid, which is what makes it delightful. It must, of necessity, be reserved for the true Austenite, the sort of person who is too often a misfit in the modern literary milieu, who spends a certain amount of time in the world of 1810, where terms like 'gentleman', 'leisure', and 'literary endeavour' have a somewhat different connotation to the ones they bear today. Readers who spend at least some of their time in this world may be tempted to take up the challenge of discovering some of my surely numerous errors – I should be delighted to hear from them.

My second enterprise was the greater, and required a greater degree of temerity than the first. Though *Mansfield Park* is often lauded as one of her two greatest works (obviously, in her case, one speaks of degrees of excellence), it is difficult to find an admirer of the novel who concurs wholeheartedly with its concluding chapters. The story has the feel of a vast and subtly orchestrated symphony which reaches a climax in a series of crashing dischords, and is then rapidly terminated with an allegretto in a minor key.

Interesting as it is to speculate on the reason for this – whether it was her incipient illness or religious conversion – it is useless to wonder whether she would eventually have rewritten the last section of this book had the events of her life permitted. As matters stand, we are left with a masterpiece in which the author seems, at the very last, to have lost interest in some of the characters. This applies particularly to the most attractive man in the book, who may, together with Henry Tilney, share the distinction of being the most attractive man in any of her books.

There is no doubt that Jane Austen knew exactly what constituted the quality of masculine attractiveness, and knew how to depict it. Henry Crawford is neither Wickham nor Willoughby, though in the original novel he certainly comes to Mansfield in search of amusement, which he takes at the expense of the Bertram sisters. He is given much more depth and humanity than his sister Mary, and though he sometimes has the same superficial facade, unlike her he is never repugnant; and when we see him in serious pursuit of Fanny, appreciating her finer qualities as no one else does at Mansfield, and modestly deprecating his own, we feel that he is worthy of something other than the outer darkness into which he is cast at the end of the story.

The problem, I think, arises partly out of our modern perception of what constitutes attractiveness. Plainly, Jane Austen intended her readers to admire Fanny while suspecting the charm of Henry Crawford, and probably to feel some satisfaction at the fate reserved for him. This does not work of course for most people today, who tend to find Fanny off-putting – too priggish and vaporish by half. She lacks the robust outspokenness of Elizabeth

Bennet, or even the sweet strength of Anne Eliot, and her main qualities of acute perception and rigid personal integrity do not endear her to our generation, whereas Henry is instantly recognisable as the sort of man mothers would still like to be able to advise their daughters against, and which it is the dream of every mousey girl to have at her feet.

Thirty years of re-reading *Mansfield Park* on a yearly basis has not shaken my conviction that at some point Jane Austen intended the union of Fanny and Henry, but that she changed her mind during the writing of it, and never had the time to revise it sufficiently, either to modify Henry's attractiveness, or the shoddy melodrama of his downfall. Today, instead of experiencing *Mansfield Park* as a commentary on the great themes of Education and Integrity, we read it for its atmosphere. As is the case with every one of her books, it opens a door into another world – we crave its order, its rationality and its sanity even when we cannot respond to its sanctities.

Mansfield Letters is intended to be read as a footnote to *Mansfield Park* – it arose from an irresistible need to rework the conclusion of the first novel in a manner that was personally satisfying. I realise that I may stir up a hornet's nest among the *cognoscenti* in my disposition of the characters thirteen years after the marriage of Fanny and Edmund, but make no apologies for this – I have dealt with them according to the needs of my story, and without stretching probability too far. I considered that Edmund, Maria and their father, having served their purpose in the original novel, were expendable, just as Mrs Norris, being inimitable, had to be got out of the way. Fanny needed to mature and mellow, and to this end motherhood and widowhood were useful devices. Henry Crawford needed weight, so he was given a profession and a career. Mary Crawford may seem a pale reflection of the witty bitch of the original – she was the hardest character to transpose, though I have softened her, as in the case of Fanny, by using the changes that are effected by time.

The chief problem in the completion of this novel was that my every reading or even reference to *Mansfield Park* was depressing – the mastery inherent in every line, every sentence, was in itself an intolerable criticism, the more implacable for its silence. When one dares to stand beside greatness, one runs the risk of total annihilation. I have needed some courage to complete this book, and to publish it. It cannot lay claim to being more than what it was initially intended to be: an intellectual exercise. But if well received, it may turn into a tribute.

Paula Atchia

PREFACE

Fanny Bertram, if asked whether or not she considered herself a favoured child of Dame Fortune, would have been somewhat taxed for a simple answer. Though on the one hand it was true that she had in childhood been taken by her uncle, Sir Thomas Bertram, from a home of poverty and discomfort, and brought up in the luxury and refinement of his home at Mansfield; and though it was also true that as a consequence she had grown into a fine young woman who had married her cousin Edmund; yet by the age of thirty one Fanny could not look back on a life of unalloyed joy and satisfaction.

Throughout the years of growing up at Mansfield Park she had felt disadvantaged in relation to her splendid cousins, and her timid and retiring manner had too frequently drawn the thunder of her truly horrible aunt Norris. This same lady had been seriously displeased at Fanny's marriage (possibly as she had taken no part in the planning of it) and she was not the type of person to suffer displeasure in silence.

Nevertheless, it was a harmonious union, for Fanny had loved Edmund for many years before the unhappy events associated with the Crawfords threw them together at last. Fanny would be the last to deny that the disappearance of Mrs Norris three years later had contributed in no small degree to their felicity, but Edmund's own premature death after only eight years together left her a widow at the age of twenty-seven, penniless and once more reliant upon her husband's family, and by now with a young son at her charge.

At the time of our story, which takes place thirteen years after the concluding events of *Mansfield Park*, Fanny had already lived four years of widowhood at Mansfield.

TIME FRAME – MAIN EVENTS
FROM 1809 TO 1822

1808 to 1809	Main action of *Mansfield Park*
Summer 1809	Marriage of Julia
Early 1810	Marriage of Fanny and Edmund
Spring 1810	Birth of Julia's first daughter
Autumn 1811	Death of Dr Grant
Spring 1812	Death of Admiral Crawford. Henry goes to India
Summer 1813	Birth of young Edmund
Autumn 1813	Tragic deaths of Sir Thomas, Maria and Mrs Norris
Winter 1814	Marriage of William
Spring 1815	Birth of Julia's second daughter
Autumn 1815	Birth of William's daughter
Summer 1817	Death of Fanny and William's father
Autumn 1818	Death of Edmund from pneumonia
Winter 1819	Birth of William's son
Spring 1820	Arrival of Dr Thwaite at Mansfield Parsonage
Autumn 1822	The present story starts

1

*T*he servants' hall at Mansfield Park had witnessed many changes in the affairs of the Bertram family since the happy time, twelve years ago, when Master Edmund had married Miss Fanny Price. The death of Dr Grant almost two years later had facilitated the move of the couple to the living at Mansfield, where young Edmund was born the following year. That autumn had come the terrific news of the deaths, by shipwreck in a hurricane, of Sir Thomas, Miss Maria and Mrs Norris, at Fort de France, on their way to Antigua.

On the occasions when this subject was canvassed downstairs, the general consensus seemed to be that though Sir Thomas was on the whole to be regretted, his eldest daughter was not; and the disappearance of Mrs Norris was greeted with such unalloyed satisfaction as would have increased the chagrin of the grieving family upstairs had they known it. Whatever the varied sentiments of the other family members had been towards the departed lady, in the servants' hall she was universally detested, and from the majestic Baddeley himself to the lowest scullery-maid the general feeling was that it was demanding too much of human nature to expect them to show a sad demeanour at the commemoration service, read so beautifully by Master Edmund.

A few of the senior servants, of course, knew the true reasons for the voyage to Antigua, and the essential facts of the scandal surrounding Miss Maria's name – beginning with her elopement with Mr Henry Crawford (him that was to have wedded Miss Fanny), and her subsequent divorce from Mr Rushworth. Baddeley himself had a nephew working over at Everingham, the Crawford seat, twenty-four miles away, so he had the information that Miss Mary had never yet been married, though she had been twice engaged to do so; and that Master Henry had departed for India a few months after the death of Dr Grant, to a life of active military service in the armies of the East India Company. What with the dangerous frontier wars, the climate, diseases and wild animals, the servants' hall had long anticipated news of his death by one or other of these agents. But they had waited in vain, and ten years later Baddeley still had no news on the subject from his nephew beyond vague rumours that Master Henry had been promoted to the rank of Major, and was soon to be married.

Four years ago the servants' hall had been shaken once more by the news of the death of Master Edmund from pneumonia, and in the general sorrowing that ensued many hoped that Master Tom would now sober down and change his style of living. Since his father's death he had been Sir Thomas Bertram, but whether from indifference or natural indolence he had not shouldered his responsibilities as head of the family, passing many of these to Edmund. The disappearance of his younger brother wrought no noticeable change in his behaviour, however; he still chose to live the life of a swell in London, only visiting Mansfield and his mother on rare occasions. He had been travelling for the past eight months in Italy, and in that time he had only twice sent a letter home to his mother – one six months ago which was simply a banker's note with an enclosed message, and the present one, received on the morning of a rainy day in early September 1822.

That night the footman was able to detail to the table downstairs that in fact *two* letters had been enclosed from Master Tom: one for her ladyship, and one for young Mrs Bertram, still generally known below stairs as Miss Fanny. Surprising as this fact was in itself, it could hardly account for the gratifying effect of these missives on the ladies – who on reading had both turned to stone – while Miss Susan had busied herself successively with hartshorn and water, smelling salts and brandy, and had finally sent for the doctor when it seemed as though her ladyship was really ill and seemed likely to faint. Mr Comyn had come, and pronounced a need for rest. This piece of medical counsel was beyond the understanding of the listening Hall, most of whom had never known Lady Bertram to walk more than a few yards from her sofa in the entire course of a day.

2

If Baddeley's nephew had been a more diligent note writer, his uncle might have guessed some part of the news by learning that Miss Mary was travelling in Italy. As it was, her ladyship remained in her room all day, closeted with her daughter-in-law, and several of the house servants would have given a week's wages to have listened to their conversation, or to become acquainted with the contents of the following letters, which I reproduce here to satisfy the curiosity of the reader:

Lombardy, 19 August '22.

Dear Mama,

I know that you will be glad to have my news, for two days ago I did something that you have been after me to do for the past ten years at least – I am married.

I do not know whether it is the sobering effect of matrimony itself now that it is come upon me, or whether it is due to the kind offices of my wife, but I feel the need to acquaint my family with my action, and solicit their welcome at Mansfield for my lady. Reasonable as this request may seem, I think you may have some second thoughts when you learn that my wife is Mary Crawford.

I saw her after many years, at Easter, in the Embassy at Rome. We renewed our acquaintance over some problems she had with her papers, met again a few days later at an Embassy party, and arranged to meet in early August at the Gordons' place in Tuscany. I had always considered Mary an admirable girl, and was from the start only kept from paying her my addresses from the conviction that she preferred Edmund. This was indeed the case, and she told me that she spent years of unhappiness on hearing first of his marriage, and more recently of his death, being quite unable to bring herself to make the usual mariage de conveniance.

You and the others at Mansfield may feel some concern at the idea of renewing ties with her and her family, especially with her brother Henry. I can tell you that the true story throws a somewhat different light on his treatment of Maria, and in any case, Maria is long dead, and Henry himself has been abroad for almost ten years. The past is the past, as the good English divine here who married us impressed upon us, and neither Mary nor myself propose to allow the past to affect our present happiness. She is my wife now, and as Mary

Bertram she must be received by my family — I count upon you to make this generally known and accepted in our circle, before we return to England next month, after our present tour. We shall begin by occupying the London house, though I would like to bring Mary to Mansfield to pay her respects to you as soon as possible.

Our united best wishes to everyone at home,

Yr. loving son,

Tom.

Although it was addressed to Fanny Bertram in Tom's handwriting, the second letter proved to be in a very different, and well-remembered hand:

La Casa Inglese,
Lombardy, 19 August.

My dear Fanny,

I once said to you that there was more than one way of our being sisters, and though I hope you still feel some affection for me as a friend, I look forward to being received by you in the near future as a sister. If you remember, I always considered you as such, have the happiest memories of you and the family at Mansfield, and have tried from time to time to follow the news of the family.

I heard of Edmund's death on a visit to Everingham last year, and the news came as a great shock. It renewed all my feelings for Mansfield, and awoke sentiments which I had considered long forgotten. I was then on the point of contracting a marriage with a very wealthy and important man in London — I daresay the echoes of it reached you. The engagement did not last long, however; sentiment (or rather the absence of it) overcame sense. It was the opposite in the case of my first engagement, five years ago, contracted in this country. In this case, sense overcame sentiment, for though Giovanni came from an ancient family, was desperately handsome, and several years younger than myself; when I realised that marriage to me was intended to restore the family fortunes, I felt obliged to cry off.

In the years between, I have thought of you, and the whole family, with so much affection, that it was with real delight that I met Tom

4

in Rome. In the midst of the usual Italian tracasserie *with papers and documents, it was good to see a Mansfield face! Moreover, the English lord accomplished in forty minutes (even with his abominable Italian) what feminine address and purity of speech had failed to achieve in two days! No more was needed. Was it so surprising that after our third meeting we decided to be content with each other, and to seek our mutual happiness together?*

I really look forward to meeting you again and renewing old ties, but this will have to wait till the whole of London has had a chance of meeting us. I will write to you from there, and in the meanwhile will end this here, as my caro sposo *seems to be nearing the end of an unusually long missive to his mother, and I still have to write to Henry.*

Yrs,

Mary Bertram.

2

*I*t was as well that the domestic staff at Mansfield knew very little of what went on in Lady Bertram's room that day, for the atmosphere there was one of unrelieved depression. Lady Bertram was not the type of wife or mother whose affections were strong enough to outlast death and years of oblivion; and if the truth were told she had reorganised her life quite conveniently after the demise of her nearest and dearest. But she knew what was expected of her in certain circumstances, and her natural indolence only rarely kept her from the performance of what she perceived as her duties. Tom's mother therefore had started out by declaring that she could never receive his wife, and in fact she no longer felt like receiving *him* either. Though her niece would not have used the same language, her sentiments were essentially very much the same, so that she felt unable to offer much constructive advice, beyond begging the lady to be calm, attempt to take some rest, and swallow some of Mr Comyn's prescriptive cordial.

She had read her own letter first, struck dumb by the implication of its opening sentence; and looking up, had seen her thought confirmed by the pale face and trembling hand of her aunt. Lady Bertram sat staring at her own missive, which she held out mutely to Fanny before falling back into the state of shock that necessitated medical attention.

Fanny read Lady Bertram's letter rapidly. She could not easily recover from the ease of manner with which this pair thus flouted the wishes of their respective families, for after what had passed thirteen years ago, was it to be expected that Mary Crawford's family would view this marriage favourably? She then remembered that Mary Crawford really had no family to speak of beyond her

6

widowed half-sister Mrs Grant, who lived in retirement somewhere in London, and her brother Henry, whose views merited no consideration, since he could be regarded by many as the root-cause of the problem between the two families. Her own cousin Tom was what he had always been – hasty, irresponsible, and totally insensitive to the feelings of others. Though in all justice, she was obliged to admit that he had the right to marry, and to bring what wife he would to Mansfield, she could not suppress the suspicion that he could be relied on to choose, of all the women in the world, the one least likely to please his mother.

The next day saw a little variation in mood and sentiment: Lady Bertram could now recollect how great a stickler Sir Thomas had always been, and how he would have reacted in these circumstances. She did not feel empowered to act against the certain wishes of her defunct spouse, even laying aside her own maternal feelings, which a sleepless night had somewhat awakened. She could now confess to a moderate desire to see her eldest born – which of course she would never satisfy – and even pronounce a certain curiosity to see how Mary Crawford would conduct herself in this interesting conjuncture.

'I do not think she would even wish to come here to Mansfield after all these years – maybe they will live in London, Fanny, or perhaps abroad? Is she not partly French?'

'I doubt she is, though I think she was educated for some time in France. I hope they may decide to settle in London, though they must visit Mansfield occasionally.' Fanny did not think it useful to add her conviction that there was no limit to the effrontery of which the new member of the Bertram family was capable. She merely concluded:

'We may not see them very often at the Park. It may be possible to arrange our yearly trips in summer to Huntingdon to coincide with their visits here.' Even as she spoke, she realised how unrealistic her suggestions were, designed to comfort the older woman rather than offer any practical course of action. She was still too shocked by the news to think clearly, but she realised that much of their conversation was either useless or irrelevant to the situation.

Lady Bertram had grown reflective: 'I am curious to see how she would behave as mistress of Mansfield. How will she be accepted by everyone? And will she ever refer to the past?' At this point it was necessary to have recourse to her handkerchief:

'Oh, Fanny, Fanny, what would poor Sir Thomas have said? Surely he would never have accepted such a state of affairs?'

Fanny was obliged to concur with the opinion of her mother-in-law on how Sir Thomas would have taken the news, though she felt more hesitant when trying to imagine how her own defunct spouse would have reacted. She knew that he had been very much in love with Mary for over a year, and only kept from marrying her by the scandal of her brother's elopement with Maria.

By this time the essential difference between the viewpoints of the two ladies lay in the fact that, unlike her aunt, Fanny felt absolutely no inclination to meet either the master of Mansfield or his new lady. She was still in a state of confusion, having lain awake half the night trying to imagine what the future held for her and her son, for to her at that stage it admitted of little doubt that she and Lady Mary Bertram could not be expected to live in the same house.

Sometime in the small hours of the morning, her mind had gone back over the years, and she found that she could remember Mary Crawford with astonishing clarity: her fragile beauty, her liveliness, grace and charm. She felt once again the jealousy her eighteen-year old self had felt at the enslavement of her cousin during that fateful summer all those years ago, when the evenings at Mansfield Parsonage were beguiled by a vision of Mary, dressed in white and seated at her harp before the French windows overlooking the twilit garden. Mary had smiled and sung, Edmund had admired and sighed, Fanny had observed and fretted inwardly. Even in those days she had known that she loved her handsome cousin, and that her freshness and innocence were as nothing compared to the brilliance of Mary.

Throughout that summer she had been the unwilling observer of this courtship, being called on occasion to share confidences with one or other of the principal parties, for to each of them 'dear Fanny' was both trusted friend and confidante. In addition to her youthful jealousy, Fanny remembered the reluctant admiration she had always felt for Mary's wit and poise, together with a certain tortured affection she could not withhold in acknowledgement of Mary's many small kindnesses to her.

But this romance was not the only one that poor green Fanny had been obliged to witness that summer. Her beautiful cousin Maria, though newly and advantageously engaged, had seen fit to throw herself at the head of Mary's elegant brother, Henry Crawford. Though this illicit courtship could not arouse the same feelings in Fanny, thirteen years later she could still remember the disagreeable nature of her sentiments whenever she unwillingly assisted at their verbal exchanges and secret glances, for some reason so clear to her, and to her only. When the final disaster struck, and the newly married Maria eloped with Henry in London, Fanny was probably the only member of the Bertram household who was not entirely stunned from surprise, although Henry had been protesting his love for herself for several months, and had gone so far as to request her hand in marriage from her uncle.

Apart from a feeling of horror, Fanny's main reaction to the news had been astonishment that a man who professed to love one woman was capable of running off with another. The intervening years at Mansfield had somewhat modified her youthful *naïveté* – she now knew that such things could and did happen, though she was not much nearer to understanding their cause. Maria's disastrous marriage had terminated in the greater disaster of her disgrace and eventual death, by which time Fanny had been too happy with her own fate to devote much thought either to her or to Henry Crawford. This last gentleman's departure for India had been tacitly acknowledged by both families as a relief, and for several years Fanny had been content to hear nothing of him, though she would not have been a normally constituted female had she not occasionally remembered him, and wondered how things would have been had she agreed to marry him all those years ago. At the present juncture, she was even less informed of his whereabouts than Baddeley.

However little conducive to restoration is a night spent in fruitless recollection, one must be thankful that the various needs of the coming day assure the continuity of daily life. The next morning Fanny could see that her aunt was in an even worse condition than herself – pale, heavy-eyed and tearful. Conversation between the two ladies at this point was restricted to exclamations of misery and lamentations from the elder, punctuated by murmurs of consolation from Fanny, and this state of affairs might have continued for the rest of the day, were it not for the appearance after breakfast of Susan. Fanny's younger sister was active, unimaginative and totally practical, which is often the necessary outlook to end fruitless reflection and induce decision-making. When Lady Bertram on seeing her burst out with:

'Oh Susan, how can we ever receive those two in this house?', her matter-of-fact reply was:

'My dear aunt, I don't see how we can refuse to receive them, considering that it is *their* house, which we occupy at *their* pleasure.'

Lady Bertram was much struck.

'That is very true, Susan, how strange of me not to have seen it before!' The idea was sufficiently animating for her to sit up in bed, and arrange her cap before making a further reflection:

'In fact, I don't suppose they even have to wait on our wishes to occupy the house; but may, if they choose, simply send us notice to quit? Oh dear, what is to become of us? Should I write to Aunt Ward in Huntingdon?'

Fanny was too busy evaluating the possible chances of these terrific eventualities to attempt to alleviate the new mood of agitation, and salvation once more came from Susan:

'Well, aunt, the first thing we have to do is to prepare for their visit. They must be housed, fed and entertained as befits the master and lady of Mansfield. Mrs Manners and the staff await your directions, and there is a visitor for you downstairs, so you must get dressed as soon as possible.'

The visitor proved to be only Dr Thwaite from the Parsonage, but for Lady Bertram his visit served two purposes: in the first place, it restored her to the land of the living, for she was obliged to leave her room and return to the drawing-room and the comfort of her sofa and fringe-basket. Secondly, the ensuing interview with the good doctor reinforced her conviction that since in the present case nothing could be done to modify her son's course of action, Christian charity was the only practical response. As is so often the case with individuals who are basically selfish, Dr Thwaite was eloquent on the subjects of charity, forgiveness and duty. Before he had spoken for thirty minutes, Lady Bertram was so far converted from her previous intolerance to acceptance of her new daughter, that had the whole of the Crawford clan presented themselves at

Mansfield in the course of the morning they would have received a charitable welcome.

As the hours passed, however, her mood wavered occasionally – although her memory was not retentive, she must have remembered at least something of the past, for during the afternoon she was observed to dry her eyes at intervals, and at dinner Fanny noticed how she frowned to herself and looked fiercely on her lamb-chop. Once from the fullness of her heart she burst out with: 'I cannot give her my hand, I cannot!' which fortunately Fanny was the only person to hear – and which created some suspense in her mind as to how her aunt would eventually welcome Tom's wife at Mansfield.

3

*D*r Thwaite had occupied the Parsonage for well over two years and had dined regularly with the family at Mansfield without very much being known of him, beyond the fact that, being possessed of independent means, he was fairly well-to-do – was an ardent Abolitionist, and was unencumbered with a wife. This was sufficient, in the opinion of his neighbours, to indicate an inclination for matrimony, and it only remained for them to identify a suitable life-partner for him. The obvious choice in this case was Fanny, who by now had been widowed for long enough to deserve a change in her condition. By popular accord, he was to be her reward. To him was to fall the pleasure of bringing up Edmund's son, and it was now several months since all the gossips in the region had felt the convenience of young Edmund's eventual inheritance of the Mansfield living.

Fanny was not totally unaware of these plans for her future felicity, though she had never given them any serious thought. An occasional look or word from the doctor had given her the idea that he concurred in this matter with popular opinion, but she thought that he was not a sufficiently courageous man to take any decided step without encouragement, and this she had scrupulously refrained from offering. Matters stood thus between them when the news of Tom's marriage reached his family and was simultaneously spread abroad, necessitating several visits of congratulation, commiseration and confabulation from neighbours and other ill-wishers. The ensuing round of social exchange was certain to involve the doctor in more than his weekly morning-call and fortnightly dinner, and this might have been an additional trial to Fanny had there not been another element in the case.

This was the doctor's nephew, a certain Mr Tilly, twenty-five years old, newly down from university and awaiting the taking of orders. As this process could take up to a year or more, he was casting about him for something to do in the meantime. He had already on occasion constituted himself as assistant to Mr Comyn, but confessed to Fanny that he lacked the stomach for surgery. This conversation had given Fanny the idea of inviting the young man to act as temporary tutor to Edmund, who at nine years old and awaiting his entry to school, had reached an age when he needed more serious instruction than he had hitherto received from Miss Lee, and was in addition in want of masculine presence and guidance.

Stephen Tilly was a pleasant young man, modest and unassuming, and if his frequent presence at the house would increase the rhythm of his uncle's visits, Fanny was prepared to put up with the inconvenience for the sake of Edmund. And not only for Edmund's sake, for she had noticed the glances that sometimes passed between Susan and the young man, at Sunday worship and on the occasions when he dined at the house with his uncle. She was not unwilling to help in promoting the happiness of a dear sister, who was otherwise in mortal danger of dying an old maid.

Susan had lived at Mansfield for the past thirteen years, and was by now as indispensable to the comfort of Lady Bertram as Fanny herself had been in the past. As strong and robust a presence as Fanny had been delicate and retiring, she was also the ideal aunt for Edmund, and it was with delight that the child welcomed an excursion with Aunt Susan, or a chance to play one of his favourite games in the grounds. Fanny realised that the tenure of her widowhood and her responsibility for Edmund had been greatly eased by the presence of this sister, the only member of her own family with whom she was in daily contact, though she often heard from her widowed mother, who still lived at Portsmouth with the youngest of her numerous children. Fanny's favourite brother William, now a ship's captain, had not been in England since the week following Edmund's funeral, although their affectionate correspondence was very regular.

Two mornings after her letter from Mary Bertram, Fanny was at her writing-table composing a letter to William, when she was interrupted by the hurried entrance of Edmund, great with news:

'Mama – such fun! Tib's kittens all have their eyes open, and Jem says that I can have the striped one, Timmy, for my own, to keep here in the house! He recognises me already, and can climb on to my shoulder – see the scratches!'

Susan, who had accompanied Edmund to the stables, came in unhurriedly, in time to intervene:

'Don't worry, Fanny, he is to come upstairs with me to get himself clean and to put ointment on that shoulder. If you don't object, I have agreed to let him keep Timmy in his room, though not for another couple of weeks. Come along, Edmund – and don't forget that you still have an hour's reading with Miss Lee, as well as yesterday's dictation to correct before luncheon!'

But Edmund was not yet done. Caressing his mother's sleeve with a very grubby hand, he addressed her winningly:

'Dear Mama, Mr Tilly says he can teach me how to bowl in the afternoons, and he has promised to bring a new cricket ball for me, as you know how Pug chewed the other one. Aunt Susan thinks that he may call this afternoon. May I come down to meet him?'

Avoiding a glance at her sister, Fanny smoothed back the ruffled curls and smiled at her son. In appearance Edmund was a typical Bertram – tall and blond – but with his mother's hazel eyes, that pleaded with her as he spoke.

'Mr Tilly is calling today to speak to me – mainly about you. If you are very good this morning, you may come down and join us for tea. But don't forget your dictation – and please darling, *quiet on the stairs!*'

The last part of her sentence was called out to her son, who had departed rejoicing loudly, followed by Susan. His mother sat listening, following their progress for several minutes before turning back to her letter.

Over the teacups that afternoon Fanny was able to reassure the bashful Mr Tilly that any help he offered with Edmund's education would be very much appreciated, and place her entirely in his debt, as it would allow Miss Lee, now over sixty, to return to her widowed sister and a second, well-merited retirement. Shortly afterwards, they were joined by Susan and Edmund, and as Fanny watched the three glowing faces around the tea-urn, she was happy to be reminded that all was not misery in the atmosphere at Mansfield.

★★★

14

So narrow was Lady Bertram's range of conversation at the best of times, that most attempts to communicate seriously with her must result either in insincerity or cruelty. In order to avoid these extremes, Fanny usually limited her exchanges with the good lady to the most trivial banalities, and in consequence all her years at Mansfield had taught her very little of the essential character of her mother-in-law.

At this time, however, she had to admit that her aunt, in a moment of extraordinary stress, showed proof of a capacity for endurance that she had displayed only twice before, on the occasion of deaths in the family. Once the initial shock of the news of Tom's marriage had passed, she developed an attitude of passivity, being heard to remark several times a day on how helpless the old were in a world dominated by the young, and how in fifty years' time it would be all the same. This laudable fatalism did not prevent her from taking steps to review certain sections of her wardrobe, and entering into several animated discussions with her maid on the need for some change of hairstyle. Reinforced on both fronts, she received with exemplary calm the news from Fanny, a week later, that the newly married couple would be at Mansfield in time for an early dinner the following day.

Fanny had no further details to offer other than the bare information, having received a scrawl of two lines from Tom in the morning, and she was consequently unable to offer any assistance either to her mother-in-law or to the rest of the household as to what preparations should be made, beyond suggesting making over the best chamber, and the preparation of some of Tom's favourite dishes for dinner.

The next day dawned wet and windy, but by mid-afternoon had cleared to autumn sunshine, so that the new mistress of Mansfield would see the house and grounds to their best advantage. From her room upstairs Fanny heard the arrival, though she was unable to do more than catch a glimpse of the carriage as it swept under the portico, and prepared herself reluctantly to go downstairs and meet Mary Bertram.

As with so many events in life that are long apprehended, the moment passed swiftly, subject to a trivial happening that swelled and absorbed all the energies of the fatal moment. Distracted

15

perhaps by her thoughts, she stubbed her foot against an irregularity in the carpet on the lowest rung of the staircase, tripped and turned her ankle. It was not a serious injury, but the stab of pain brought tears for an instant, and in the effort of straightening herself, testing her foot, and walking carefully into the drawing-room, she passed over her larger apprehensions.

She heard Mary's trilling laugh and her voice even before she saw her: 'Tom's opinion of his horses can only be compared with my rating of my cook – too often performance cannot equal expectation. You must have been awaiting us this past hour at least!'

Lady Bertram was answering in a low voice, and she had given the new family member her hand and her cheek, so that for the moment the worst was over. Breathing her relief, Fanny was able to smile and nod at both Tom and his wife, and even exchange a sisterly embrace with Mary, before standing back and trying to distinguish the changes time had wrought upon her new relative.

These were heavy. The slim, light silhouette of youth had matured into the embonpoint of maturity, and though her clear olive complexion and luxuriant dark curls were unchanged, Mary at thirty-three undoubtedly had more presence than she had ever possessed at twenty. To Fanny's imagination, her voice seemed different – it was louder and more penetrating, with a husky undertone that Fanny could not remember. The laugh had not changed though, and neither had her poise and sense of humour – Mary would always be mistress of any situation she found herself in, and she certainly was in this one; dimpling and smiling, indefatigably gracious and calmly superior.

She paid special attention to Fanny, greeting her with delight, and even warm affection. Fanny was kindly remembered as a charming adolescent, grown prettier with age, as which of us does not? She seemed to remember only what she chose to, and one could not but admire her presence and spirit as she remarked on how little Fanny had changed, 'still so youthful after all these years, and ten – no, eight – years of marriage!'

It would have been easy for Fanny to forget that she stood here in the presence of the woman who had once loved Edmund, and expected to become his wife. It was even harder to recollect that this was Henry Crawford's sister, with all the painful memories associated with the name.

Mary's charm extended beyond the immediate family circle. Soon it was Baddeley's turn to be nodded, smiled and dimpled at, with a kindly allusion to the good work his nephew was doing at Everingham, and the high opinion her brother had of him.

At this indirect allusion to her 'infamous brother', Fanny saw Lady Bertram raise her eyes to heaven. Tom, however, was obviously of the same opinion as his parson on the matter of Christian charity and forgiveness, for a few moments later, looking out over the evening lawns, he initiated the topic of re-designing the grounds at Mansfield. Turning to Fanny with a reminiscent smile, he asked whether she could remember Henry's early attempts in that line, at Sotherton. Blushing painfully, and scarcely knowing where to look, Fanny murmured that she 'could not recollect – so much time had passed,' and attempted to change the subject. Though Tom had never been remarkable as a sensitive soul, he seemed to have grown worse with time, and even to have acquired some of the effrontery of his spouse, for he did not easily abandon the topic, and Fanny owed her comfort eventually more to Baddeley's announcement of dinner than to the combined efforts of Susan and his wife.

Not surprisingly, in bed that night Fanny lay sleepless for an hour, subject to a dull headache. She tried to blot out the events of the evening, but certain passages would intrude – one in particular returning over and over again. It occurred after dinner, in the drawing-room, when the tea-tray had been brought in. Mary had manoeuvred a place beside Fanny, and engaged her in a low-voiced conversation, the main aim of which seemed to be to extract from her a promise of 'getting together for a comfortable chat', which by this time the slightly overwrought Fanny could not but see as something of a threat. Mary concluded by promising her new relation a visit to her room that very night, for the promised exchange. Fanny had to exert a last effort to persuade her that she was far too tired to talk – and consequently postpone the moment for the next night, to which she realised she was now committed. Fanny's high degree of delicacy made it difficult for her to imagine what Mary wanted to discuss with her, but in the course of the evening she had realised that there was probably no subject that Mary would shrink from examining with her new cousin.

The newly wedded couple were not at breakfast the next morning, and it was well past midday when Mary entered the drawing-room – preceded by her laugh – and followed by Edmund, who was to all intents and purposes already her follower.

'Fanny, this child says he has never sat on a horse! I'm sure you will not mind if he comes out with me one morning when the weather is fine, and we get Jem to saddle one of the quieter horses for him. Do you remember how it was when I was learning to ride?'

Fanny remembered only too well – long mornings spent waiting for her horse, while Mary rode out in the sunshine with Edmund and his sisters, who were naturally attended by Henry. Their laughter from the lower meadow had on occasion penetrated as far as the house, where Fanny toiled at gardening or other household chores, supervised by Aunt Norris, while Lady Bertram dozed gently on her sofa. It was perhaps a pang from the past that prompted her to reply:

'Of course I do, and how kind of you to offer to teach him! But I have just arranged with Mr Tilly, who is to come three days a week to supervise his lessons – and on these days will stay after luncheon to help with things like riding and cricket in the afternoons.'

So that was that, and Mary immediately turned her attention elsewhere. But Fanny could see that Edmund was going to hang on to his uncle's wife during her visit, and that Mary was not so completely immune to flattery, even from such a very youthful admirer, as to ignore him completely.

At dinner that night Fanny assisted at a brief exchange between Mary and her mother-in-law which further convinced her that times had changed at Mansfield. The conversation opened trivially enough, with an idle remark from Mary on the colour of the dining-room curtains, which Lady Bertram informed her were considerably faded from their original gold to a soft cream. They had worn remarkably well, she added, having been ordered by Sir Thomas from Belgium in the year after Julia's birth.

' – but so fine is the quality of the cloth that, apart from the natural dimming of the colour, they are still as good as new, though we had them re-lined last year. Why do you ask?'

Mary appeared to reflect for a few seconds before she answered.

'I can see that you will be of invaluable assistance to me when I start the business of re-furnishing. Though not for the moment, of course – this visit is more in the nature of a *tour d'inspection*!'

There was something in her expression as she spoke, something in the curl of her lip and the toss of her curls that convinced Fanny that the present truce was not destined to last for long. She took this thought up to bed with her, and it stayed with her while her hair was being brushed and after her maid was dismissed.

It was still somewhere at the back of her mind when she heard Mary's tap at the door, and saw her enter and place her candle on the commode before looking about her. Standing in the candle-light, with the heavy shawl thrown over her nightgown and her hair cascading down her back, she looked more like the youthful Mary of the past than the sophisticated matron of the dinner-table. There was a naughty smile on her face as she exclaimed:

'So this used to be Maria's room! I don't envy her taste in furniture.'

Then, turning towards Fanny and still smiling: 'Dear Fanny! I thought the evening would never end, and cards are so boring! What is more, I suspect *belle-maman* and Thwaite of a conspiracy – I doubt whether she is intelligent enough to cheat, but his cards fell remarkably well and *toujours à propos* – did you notice? But we have so much to talk about, I seem to have spoken so often to you in my thoughts, these past few years.'

Fanny did not remark that she had lived the same experience, particularly since hearing the news of Tom's marriage. Instead she stood waiting beside the dresser, nervously rearranging the candle-sticks, watching Mary move forward to settle herself at the head of the bed, pulling out pillows and propping herself comfortably before turning towards her reluctant hostess, evidently preparing for a long and intimate conversation.

4

'Put that candle down, Fanny – come and sit here by me – I need to see you properly. How strange that you have changed so little in so many years!' Mary seemed to be talking as much to herself as to Fanny.

'Tom says that he prefers me now – but should a wife ever believe the word of a husband? But in your case – I think it must be your expression – you still seem half-apprehensive and afraid to talk, looking as though you would like to run away when someone addresses you directly. Seeing you like this today is the strangest thing! I seem to have gone back into the past – to those days when my life's happiness seemed so close, and the terrible news came from Wimpole Street to spoil everything.' Here she hesitated, as though giving Fanny a chance to say something, and when this did not happen she continued:

'I wrote Henry many letters at the time for I did not know exactly what had happened – but he did not answer me. In fact, I never knew the full story till much later, when he learned of your marriage, and wrote me a long letter, full of bitterness.'

There was another slight pause before she went on:

'As you can imagine, I felt some bitterness about the event on my own account – and did not reply to him for several weeks. By then I had heard reports from some of our mutual friends concerning his excesses and the life he lived, usually in the company of our uncle. He went completely wild – for a time we almost feared for his sanity. The Admiral's death more than a year later, and his own decision to depart for India, seemed to steady him. I saw him several times in London just before he left. He was very calm by then, and spoke of Mansfield, and especially of you and Edmund, with detachment. He never mentioned Maria by name – though I knew he still felt intense resentment towards her.'

Fanny once more forbore reflection, this time on the degree of resentment that Maria's family was surely entitled to feel towards the man who had seduced and ruined her. Yet even as the thought entered her mind, she recalled scenes from the Mansfield theatricals of that past summer, and in justice she was obliged to admit that to the discerning observer it had been Maria who had pursued Henry Crawford, and not the other way around.

She could recall scenes and incidents which still had the power to make her blush for shame at Maria's behaviour. Even to the naive adolescent that was Fanny at eighteen, barely aware of her own awakening feelings for Edmund, Maria's infatuation for Henry had been clear enough, though Fanny had never understood its intensity, or what the engaged girl saw in Henry Crawford. Even less had she understood a few months later why the newly married Maria had consented to elope with him, bringing chaos down on both their families.

In the years following her own marriage, on the few occasions she had recalled these events or discussed them with her husband, she found herself inclined to place a greater responsibility for precipitating the final disaster on the lady than on the gentleman. Though it was true that Henry Crawford was guilty of egotism and vanity in his relations with the Bertram sisters, he had shown generosity and sensitivity in his relations with other people; whereas Maria, brought up to consider her own will as law by her mother and aunt, and forced into hypocrisy by the severity of her father, had never had to surmount temptation, or to consider the superior rights of another in any relationship.

Fanny was startled out of a half-dream of reflection by Mary's voice: 'Did you ever hear the whole story of what really happened at Richmond?'

'No – not really – I only know what Edmund heard and told me at the time. He did not find it an easy subject to discuss, and it was impossible to broach the subject with Sir Thomas, naturally.'

'Edmund knew very little, only what I had told him in our last interview, when I myself knew almost none of the real facts of the case. The truth was that Maria had been mad for Henry from the start, and her marriage had only exacerbated her sentiments, for it awoke a sensuality that it could not satisfy. To make things worse, she heard of his love for you and it exasperated her. While we were together in London, I witnessed two of their meetings, and saw her pursuit of him – reckless and shameless!' – here she paused, a scornful expression on her face.

'In fact, his entire *affaire* with her – if one can use such a word for a single night spent together – was her own doing. One evening I watched him try to ignore her, tease her, and finally turn on her in impatience and anger. She wept and clung to his arm; there were eight other people present at the time, but Maria was lost to what people might think! In the carriage on our way home he swore to me that he would never see her again. I was glad, for I genuinely wanted him to marry you. We both felt relief at the end of our association with her in her present state, but we had not reckoned with her desperation.' Mary changed position against the pillows and looked directly at Fanny for the first time since she had started speaking.

Fanny stared back reluctantly, mesmerised by past feeling. She could recall the evening when she first heard the news of the elopement – sitting in her father's house in Portsmouth and listening to him read out a paragraph from the newspaper.

'She got him to visit her one evening at her friend's house in Richmond, by sending him a note saying that she had heard from you – that you were in some trouble and had appealed to her. He knew how miserable you were at Portsmouth, and in Edmund's absence how friendless. He rushed to see Maria, anticipating the joy of bringing you back to Mansfield within three days.' Here Mary stopped and stared into the candle for some moments, and her lips tightened. Fanny felt almost sick with remembered emotion, but a dreadful fascination held her silent and listening.

'The scene was well set for seduction – Henry never stood a chance. Maria, more beautiful since her marriage, more abandoned, more desperately in love with him, literally threw herself at him.' Mary paused once more, and she and Fanny both stared at the candle for a few moments. Fanny once more asked herself the question: how it was that a man professedly in love with one woman could yield to the shallow seductions of another? Mary seemed to sense the question, and to have no problem supplying the answer:

22

'He had been too faithful to you, Fanny, and for too long. Henry's is not a nature that can tolerate a too-long abstention from his pleasures, and I learned later that he had even given up all his little "interests" in London for your sake. It was to have been a completely new beginning – except that you had never given any answer, or allowed him to hope in any way, and Maria was half naked in his arms, pleading with him! He never claimed to be a saint, Fanny, and I agree with him that some forms of virtue are as harsh as cruelty. He told me later that he left her as soon as he could, making her promise secrecy, and swear never to meet again.'

Here Fanny had to say something: 'But they did – meet again! They lived together in London for several weeks – '

Mary interrupted: 'No, that is the point, they did not. At first Maria bombarded him with hysterical letters and messages to which he did not reply. Finally she quarrelled with her mother-in-law, actually admitting adultery to her, and to her husband – exulting in it, throwing it in their faces before walking out. You knew of that?'

Fanny nodded, finding it impossible to speak.

'Henry had a small apartment in town, known only to a few of his cronies, where he had gone on leaving our uncle's house. I think he may have had some notion of hiding from her, and cannot think how she discovered its existence, but she turned up there that day with nothing but a portmanteau, declaring she had left her husband. They quarrelled dreadfully. He wanted her to leave immediately, to return to her husband, to go to Mansfield, to go anywhere. She raved, and swore never to leave him. He told me in his letter, that at that point he considered killing her, or himself. He did neither, of course, but left her there, and drove all night and the next day to Everingham, mad with despair. He never saw her again, though she stayed there, in his rooms, for several weeks, writing him desperate letters, trying to get him to marry her – '

Once more, Fanny had to speak: 'But everyone thought they were together! Even Maria, when she wrote to Julia – '

Mary laughed. 'Maria's pride! Could she really admit to living alone for so long in Henry's rooms? But the staff there and at Everingham knew the truth, as did at least two of Henry's friends.'

23

Fanny interrupted once more: 'But you yourself wrote me a letter, mentioning that Henry had just returned from Richmond – '

Mary smiled bitterly: 'Another of my lies discovered! But my intentions at least were pure: I suspected something of what was going on, and my aim was to allay any hint of suspicion on your side. I knew how much he needed you, and how unimportant was his involvement with her. When he escaped to Everingham, I had no way of knowing what was passing, informed as I was only by our mutual friends, out to make mischief.'

There was another short pause before Mary concluded: 'Finally she was persuaded to leave London by her father, and as you know, was settled in the North with Mrs Norris, but her behaviour over there was even harder to control. As you also know, the trip to Antigua was decided upon much later, after four scandalous years, when her mother learned from Mrs Norris that Maria was expecting a child.'

This was a bit of information that had never been breathed outside the family circle, and it startled Fanny to hear Mary mention it so casually.

'Don't look so shocked, Fanny. It was Henry himself who mentioned it to me in a letter – it seems the gentleman was an acquaintance of his. Unfortunately, he was already married, else poor Maria might have found some peace at last.'

'I hope she *has* found peace at last, which is all any of us can hope to find. My uncle had further business over there, and we all hoped that in a new society, in a different part of the world, she and her child would be accepted, if they were handsomely provided for. But this was not to be, alas.'

'And alas for poor Mrs Norris, who had always nursed such fears for the death of Sir Thomas by shipwreck!' This was said with a sly roguish smile, before Mary turned serious once more. 'Still, it must have been a dreadful shock for the family when the news came?'

'Yes, it was.' Looking back over the tragic moments of her young life, Fanny still found it difficult to evaluate the relative force and weight of some events; she had never decided, even to herself, whether Maria's shocking elopement or her tragic death had been harder to bear, at the time. She went on: 'In fact, for several weeks it seemed as though my aunt Bertram would not long survive her husband. She suffered a severe heart-attack a week later, and for over a month she was completely bed-ridden.'

'A sofa-ridden woman became bed-ridden!' Mary declared with satisfaction, and though Fanny had never appreciated Mary's conversational style, she could not help a stab of amusement.

She continued, 'It was a terrible time for the whole family. Fortunately, Lady Bertram had her sons, and a daughter, to comfort her.'

'And a daughter-in-law to do all the running of errands! Why not admit it, Fanny? You must have been the ideal daughter! But, tell me, that was not the reason why you married Edmund, was it, to be of constant service to his mother?'

Fanny needed time to adjust to the shift in topic. She had never before imagined this part of the conversation, and sought for words that would not hurt Mary: 'I'm afraid I was as much shocked by the news as anyone, and if any of us was put upon at the time, it was Susan. She did all the running, not just at the time, but for months afterwards.'

Mary was gazing at her intently. 'Fanny, you have not answered my question.'

Fanny drew in a long breath. 'Edmund – Edmund had always been my best – we had been friends from childhood. After I left my family and came to Mansfield, he took the place of a brother. I never saw William again till we were grown, I loved Edmund.' Her voice grew still softer, 'We loved each other sincerely – '

Mary gave a nervous laugh: 'Did you never feel that you had married a brother, that your relations were somehow incestuous? How shocked you look, Fanny. It is obvious that you have had no direct speaking at Mansfield for too long. Don't worry, I won't tease you any more. I always thought that you and Edmund had simply consoled each other for the damage done to your lives by the Crawfords.'

She was leaning forwards as she spoke; her eyes shone in the candle-light, her flushed cheeks shaded by the glossy midnight curls. She raised her hand to the light, to admire her hoop of gold.

'Life is so strange, is it not? I can remember how I planned to marry Tom after our first dinner here with the Bertrams! My motives then, of course, were of the basest – he was handsome, rich and titled. Here at Mansfield I learned how to value people differently, but what did it serve me in the end? My feeling for Edmund, and his for me – ' She stopped and there was a pause of some length and intensity: Fanny felt her heart beating at her throat. The silence increased, till broken by Mary, speaking very gently: 'Tell me, please, about his death. Where were you at the time?'

Fanny had been half-dreading this, and was better prepared to answer, though it was hard to keep her voice steady while she spoke:

'We were at the Parsonage, here at Mansfield. As you may guess, Edmund took all his duties very seriously, especially that of visiting the sick. The weather had been bad for days, yet he could not be persuaded to stay home and rest a bad cold – someone was dying two miles away, so he had to be off. His horse lost a shoe, and they limped home very late that night in a downpour, with Edmund feverish and already delirious – it seems they had been wandering in the dark for hours.' Both women stared into the candle-light for some moments before Fanny continued:

'He slipped into a coma the next evening, though both doctors in attendance had tried everything. He only recovered conscious-ness three days later, just hours before – he passed away. He spoke very clearly to his son and to me, to his mother and to Julia, who had travelled from London. Tom arrived for the funeral, he had not received our messages in time.'

There was another silence, before Fanny concluded: 'I lived at the Parsonage till Dr Thwaite's appointment. He has been a great comfort to us all.'

Mary grimaced slightly: 'You know my sentiments, in general, for the cloth. But Edmund – I can never forget what he was to me, nor my deception at his loss. Sometimes, with Tom, I like to imag-ine he is Edmund – ' She broke off suddenly and smiled brilliantly at Fanny: 'I think, on the whole, I was well served for my pride and ambition, and am fortunate indeed to still be able to call myself Lady Bertram at last!'

Fanny could not reply. Mary had not changed, she was still the same capricious mixture of sincerity and artifice, of affection and selfishness, that had baffled and repelled her in the past. Fanny could not like her as a person any better than she ever had, but she was beginning to know her slightly better, and must learn in time to accept her.

5

*U*pon Mary's departure Fanny slept immediately and heavily, but in the days that followed she recalled this conversation many times, and somewhat to her annoyance found that she could remember whole passages verbatim. Having for so many years simply assumed Henry Crawford's guilt in his 'affair' with Maria, she had some difficulty adjusting her ideas around the proposition that he was in this case more sinned against than sinning; though she reassured herself that his general behaviour, particularly with regard to her cousins, had been cynical and decadent in the extreme.

But in her case? How could one qualify Henry Crawford's behaviour towards the youthful Fanny Price? Although Fanny had no greater advantages than her youth and innocence, and although he had visited her home at Portsmouth and met her family (here Fanny blushed painfully, even in retrospect), he had fallen in love with her so deeply as to overlook every material disadvantage of the match and to honourably request her hand in marriage from her uncle. It was only after several months of unsuccessful courtship that he had removed to London, where he had met Maria once more, with disastrous consequences.

Mary's explanation for her brother's fall from grace somehow rang true. Charming, wealthy and spoiled, Henry had never been without his *menus plaisirs*, provided by a whole entourage of adoring women – his attitude towards her cousins had been more a casual acceptation of their homage than any active pursuit. Fanny herself was probably the first girl to have been unmoved by his courtship.

Had she really been totally unmoved? Looking back at that summer, she could remember that although she had at no moment considered accepting his proposals, and although she had failed to understand his attraction for both her cousins; she had definitely modified her opinion of him as time passed and he appeared genuine in his sentiments and resolute in his desire to change his way of life. However, she had never given him the smallest reason to hope for their eventual marriage, in despite of considerable pressure put on her by everyone at Mansfield – including Edmund, who had no notion of her secret feelings for himself. Trying to remember Henry, she had some difficulty recalling his face, though she could remember a lithe presence, a very charming smile, and a voice reading Shakespeare one afternoon in the drawing-room while even her aunt forgot to doze on her sofa.

At present she was inclined to admit to herself the partial truth, at least, of Mrs Norris' assertion that 'Fanny was the cause of it all.' With the passage of time, she could see more clearly how some minor part of the responsibility for Maria's failed marriage could be attributed to her, in that had she given Henry the slightest encouragement he would perhaps have been proof against Maria. But would he? Were not both Crawfords so anchored in selfish egotism, and holding such false values, that any relationship between them and the inhabitants of Mansfield was doomed to failure? Yet here was this present marriage ...

Fanny was recalled from her reverie by the voice of her aunt, gently requesting a new pen. Looking at Lady Bertram bent over her writing-tray, Fanny thought that she could see fresh signs of dissatisfaction on her face. She knew that there had been several minor disagreements between the erstwhile mistress of Mansfield and her new daughter, for she had been on the receiving end of confidences from both ladies.

Only yesterday morning Lady Bertram had murmured against Mary's attitude towards herself: she was disrespectful, uncaring of Mansfield and its residents, and generally seeking to supplant her. This sort of complaint being so out of character, Fanny felt obliged to commiserate with her aunt, and was only mildly surprised when Mary in turn got her to walk (with her and her now habitual courtier, Edmund) in the garden after tea. She complained of their mother-in-law in more vigorous terms: she was 'cold and unfriendly, most uncooperative, and generally rated her dog higher than anyone else at Mansfield'.

Nevertheless, they did have many points in common. Each claimed that the other was basically a selfish person, lazy, incompetent, and generally unfit for her station. If this was insufficient, each claimed that the other was the least amiable person of her acquaintance.

Despite some small degree of apprehension at finding herself thus stationed in the line of crossfire, so to speak, Fanny could not refrain from an inward smile at the general similitude of mind between two ladies whose outer aspects were so strikingly different. They seemed to her to have just as many points of resemblance as of difference, though neither of them would have appreciated this, and she could imagine the indignation with which any such suggestion would have been received by either.

However slight, the strains inherent in this state of affairs at Mansfield were soon apparent to more people than Fanny. Even though the new master's visit was intended to be a short one, it was barely a week into their stay before Tom and Mary were declaring that they had met all the more amiable people of the neighbourhood, and were casting about for an agreeable scheme that would remove them from Mansfield, were it only for a day.

The original idea was for a picnic which would take in a visit to a great house nearby, and ensure a return drive by moonlight to late supper. A prolonged spell of bad weather, however, relegated this project to the following summer. Several mornings at breakfast were then devoted to discussing alternative outings and trips of pleasure, but nothing was decided on until Tom mentioned one morning that he had been talking to his estate-manager, who was considering the introduction of some of the new agricultural practices coming into fashion. He had heard that Henry, although absent from England, had approved the implementation of many of these at Everingham, and he was interested in visiting the place sometime and seeing how things went on over there.

Mary supported her husband with enthusiasm, taking his idea even further: 'Certainly you must go, dearest, and while you are about it, why not take Fanny and myself for an outing? We need not spend above one night there – or at most two – and it will be most interesting to visit the house once again. I have not been there for nearly a year!'

A very few minutes' exchange served to complete every minor detail of the trip; which since Tom needed to be in Town the following week, could not take them to Everingham for more than one night, as they had not yet completed their duty-visits around Mansfield.

It only remained to inform Fanny of her good luck, which upon her entering the breakfast-parlour, the benevolent pair immediately proceeded to do.

Fanny's first reaction was one of astonishment. 'Everingham! Why, it must be more than halfway to King's Lynn! Why not choose somewhere closer for a day's outing?'

Tom was adamant. 'The distance is under twenty-three miles, or four hours with a good team. We can easily arrange to spend the night there and return the following day, which will be better for the horses. Mary wants to see the house again, and I would like to talk to Barton, the estate-manager, about some changes I am planning at Mansfield.'

Fanny said no more, till she realised that both her cousin and his wife assumed that she was to be one of the party. It then turned out that one of the ostensible purposes of the expedition was to cheer the widow in her sorrow and solitude, and neither of them could see any good reason why Fanny might be reluctant to visit the place. Upon reflection, Fanny could see why it was unfair of her to expect delicacy of feeling from either of the parties concerned.

The subject was mooted daily at every meal for two days, till finally, when Fanny saw that even her aunt and Susan were ranged against her, she decided to review her position. It was not merely that Tom really wished to obtain necessary information at Everingham for his projected improvements at Mansfield; she thought it was probably also an elegant way for him to indicate to his new brother-in-law that the past was buried as far as he was concerned, since his marriage to Mary. The meeting between the two men, whenever it took place, was bound to be awkward; and here was an action which might serve to dissipate some of the stored resentment that might be still existent. Being provided with an excuse for the trip to Everingham, she could now inwardly admit to a real curiosity to see the house of which she had almost become mistress. This was probably her only chance to do so, as Mary thought that Henry might return to England with his bride, after completing his present tour of duty.

She therefore allowed herself to be persuaded to accompany the pair. The Wednesday of the following week was decided on, and a message dispatched to Everingham informing of their visit. Both Tom and his wife would have preferred a longer stay than the single night which was all they had the time for, but since they proposed leaving for London the day after their return to Mansfield, this was not possible. Fanny could only be thankful.

She was also aware of a growing sense of expectancy associated with this outing. The tenor of her life at Mansfield was of necessity very circumscribed – she had been to London twice during the years of her marriage, and since then the yearly expedition to Huntingdon constituted her only opportunity for travel. She could not suppress some feeling of excitement at the idea of movement, of travel to an interesting place, and in such agreeable company. As a conversationalist, Mary had lost none of her charm, and her stories about her extensive circle of fashionable friends provided someone like Fanny with rare entertainment.

Resigned as she now was to the expedition, she sustained a shock on Tuesday morning at breakfast when Mary was handed a letter with an Italian postmark, written in a remembered hand.

'From Henry! But how wonderful, I haven't heard from him for months!' Mary exclaimed over the misdirections, the postmark and the date (for it had been posted in Genoa in early August) before opening it and quickly perusing its contents, with two more exclamations to herself while doing so. She then turned to her husband and announced:

'He is almost halfway home, it seems, and must have been in Genoa at about the same time that we left Rome. He plans to spend late summer with a friend in Lombardy, and should be in England by – which month are we?'

'Today is the first of October,' said Fanny.

'Ah, yes. By the middle of this month … looks forward to seeing us in London sometime in November – hum, quite a lot of news.'

Tom was already launched into a diatribe on the inefficiency of the Italian postal system, the insalubrity of Italian inns, and the indigestibility of Italian food, and hardly heard his wife's remarks, much less observed the effect the letter appeared to have on his cousin.

Fanny sat appalled. She had not yet decided what attitude to adopt to Mary's problematic brother, but she could not help but see how impossible it would be to differ once more from the rest of the family, as she had in the past, over this particular person. She shrank instinctively from seeing him again, and had even decided on more than one occasion to refuse him the meeting, though she knew that practically, in social terms, this was impossible.

Ignored by the others, Fanny sat on in meditation, alternately blushing and shivering. What if he was already on his way to England? What if he arrived at Everingham during their stay? Although she knew this to be extremely unlikely as he was not expected in the country for at least another fortnight, she felt almost sick at the thought of a sudden confrontation. She remembered their last parting in Portsmouth, when he had held her hand over-long and kissed it several times, his eyes on her face. He had seemed genuinely sorry at their separation and very much in love with her, and his affectionate messages sent through Mary seemed to confirm this view – but what had transpired? His rumoured elopement with Maria, and their presumed seclusion together for several weeks before her family could persuade her to leave him.

Mary's midnight conversation with her had certainly shed new light on this behaviour, but it could not totally exonerate him, nor decrease her reluctance to see him again. The next day's excursion had now lost all charm for her, and she found herself hoping that bad weather might render a change of plan necessary. But Wednesday morning dawned perversely bright and clear, there were no setbacks at breakfast, and they set out from Mansfield some time before noon.

6

*E*ither Tom's judgement was at fault, or the performance of his present team far inferior to those of the past, for the journey took much longer than the projected four hours. Even though their unique stop for refreshment – at Grantham – did not exceed half an hour, it was early sunset when they drove past the lodge gates of Everingham, and so weary were they that not even Fanny had the heart to remark the beauty of the autumnal woods in the twilight. The lighted house seemed a haven of rest after the long hours of jolting on the dusty road, and as she alighted Fanny could think of nothing but a wash, a change of clothes, and something hot to eat before bedtime. She had turned to speak her thanks to the coachman when the door of the house opened, so that she started up the stone staircase behind the others, and had actually climbed three of the steps before she looked up into the open doorway and met the eyes – not of the butler or the housekeeper, but of the owner himself.

It was a moment of surprise for all, and shock for at least one. While Fanny clutched the balustrade and Tom searched for words, Mary was the first to speak, running up the stairs and embracing her brother warmly: 'Why, Henry, how marvellous! When did you arrive? We did not look to see you for several weeks! Let me look at you – you look older – '

Then followed the exclamations, congratulations, handshakes and cordiality that will always accompany any reunion of family and friends after a long separation; more pronounced perhaps when there is some doubt as to the precise degree of amity involved, or where the friendship has weathered some considerable strain in the recent past. This was pretty much the present case; fortunately there seemed little for Fanny to do but to shake hands and stand silently listening to Mary's raptures as she hung fondly upon her brother. These were ably seconded by her husband, to which Henry responded in a somewhat restrained tone.

The first topic of conversation, naturally, was the nuptials of Tom and Mary, and after an adequate amount of comment and felicitation, the next subject laughingly broached was their host's present unexpected appearance in his own house. This subject he seemed disposed to banish as quickly as possible, merely remarking on opportune weather and travelling conditions overland from Genoa:

'Which is why I was lucky enough to arrive yesterday morning in good time to welcome you all today, instead of kicking my heels in a bug-infested hostelry in Belgium. But it feels so good to be home!'

Here he paused for a long moment and looked out over the darkening woods before continuing, 'Especially in autumn, all the sweeter for its contrast with the heat and odours of these past months. I have been travelling since early June, in regions where light, sound and odour seem more designed to shock than to soothe. But come' – here he seemed to recollect himself – 'let us go in.'

He waved them into the house, walking beside Fanny as Tom led Mary indoors:

'Welcome to Everingham.' He looked directly at Fanny as he spoke, and smiled at her for the first time. His voice was low: 'You have not spoken as yet to me, not to say anything ... Am I welcome?'

Here Fanny felt the impossibility of answering otherwise than in gentle assent. 'Certainly you are,' with an effort at a half-smile and relief at joining the others in the Hall, where the housekeeper waited.

When the door of her room finally closed on her, Fanny found herself able to think at last, though she still felt as though she moved through the mist of a dream or nightmare. Sinking into a chair, she ran over in her mind the events of the past half-hour. Repeatedly she looked up into the remembered face and felt the sick jolt of amazement and apprehension, but she could go no further. Had he felt the same surprise? He had obviously been expecting them, but was he pleased to see them? Certainly, his welcome had been warm, but remembering his address and the power of his charm, she could not be sure of his sincerity. Surely he felt some embarrassment at seeing her again? Would he say as much to his sister, with whom he was obviously closeted somewhere? Over and over again she regretted her decision to visit Everingham, the unlucky chance that they had not scheduled their journey forty-eight hours earlier. She almost trembled at the thought of sitting at supper with him, of the effort involved in making conversation. Of what were they to talk? To her feverish mind, there seemed an embargo on every topic. What if – what if he thought she was seeking him out with some vulgar widow's design? Almost thankfully, she remembered his projected marriage.

She could not remember whether she had first heard of it from Mary or from Tom, but she remembered feeling slightly surprised over the fact that he had waited so long to marry. It was only the third or fourth time she had heard his news in the intervening years since their last meeting, and she had thought of him, if at all, as long-married, perhaps with children. She could now confess to some curiosity as to the reason for this belated marriage, and the personality of the woman who had succumbed to Henry's bruising style of courtship. Did she consider herself fortunate? Was she even now in London deep in the business of bridal clothes? What did she look like – was she young? And what –

The clock on the landing outside her room struck seven, recalling Fanny to the need of preparing for supper, and of the futility of her present reflections.

***

An hour later, Fanny found herself seated alone in the drawing-room, but not for long. Mary came tripping downstairs with the news that the men had been closeted for over an hour with Henry's estate-manager, and would very likely be late for supper. Fanny silently commended Tom, at least, on getting done some of what he had ostensibly set out to do, and vocally hoped for good weather on the morrow for their return, which she thought should not be delayed, in view of the unexpected length of the journey. Mary was in good spirits, and informative on this point:

'We leave after early lunch, and with a team of Henry's horses I wager I will be back at Mansfield in time for dinner. Henry desired us to stay, but Tom has an appointment in London on Friday. Henry leaves for town in a few days, and we shall meet him there.' She broke out suddenly: 'Wasn't it a surprise seeing him so unexpectedly – and after all these years? You looked as though you might fall down the stairs!' She laughed musically, 'And Henry – he went so white! – I thought for a moment he was ill!'

Fanny did not really know how to reply to this, and could only murmur something about 'a momentary awkwardness, soon over', before Mary gave another trill – 'Oh dear Henry, he is so *drôle*! You know, I really think he feels a certain *gêne* at meeting you again – imagine, you who have been married for years and borne a child – I think he is probably the more innocent of the two!'

It was left to Fanny to reflect that her years of marriage to the high-minded Edmund could hardly have given her the worldly experience or sophistication to match the reckless and dissipated mode of life, which by some accounts had been Henry's, in the years since their last meeting.

Mary was looking around the room appreciatively. 'This room is as lovely as ever, with those long windows overlooking the South Lawn. It only wants completely new furnishing to be perfect.'

At last Fanny was able to smile, and comment on the pleasant task ahead for Henry's new bride.

Mary turned to look at her, eyebrows raised in surprise. 'What bride – did you not know? Henry's marriage has been cancelled, which is probably why he is back in England so early. He mentioned it in his last letter, but gave no details.' She turned towards the pianoforte. 'It's a pity there's no harp here, but there used to be a book of my favourite waltzes and mazurkas in the piano seat – ah, here it is, and here are some sonatas – ' and seating herself she was immediately busy with the remembered notes, leaving Fanny to her thoughts, or rather to her renewed state of confusion.

She began resolutely by emphasising to herself that Henry Crawford's marital intentions were none of her affair. The man had every right to return to his homeland after long years abroad in the service of his country, and reside in his own house, without reference to her or to anyone else. She repeated this admirable conclusion over and over to herself, but it could not keep her from a feeling of profound unease.

She could not help remarking to herself how awkward this new piece of information might prove to the general scheme of things: that a returned Henry Crawford, newly and suitably married, was far more socially digestible than a Henry Crawford who was an ex-suitor and reprobate. Could it be that he would be received at Mansfield? At this point Fanny was forced to give herself a mental shake. In view of who the present master was, and the identity of his new wife, and the new order that was to prevail, how could he not be? Not for the first time since the news of Tom's marriage, Fanny was forced to envisage a near future away from Mansfield, living somewhere quietly, perhaps in Huntingdon or even London, with Lady Bertram and Susan.

Mary was still working away at her sonata, with Fanny seated in a state of tolerable distraction looking through a newspaper, when the gentlemen entered, full of apologies for their lateness. Tom was in high spirits – in good humour with his brother-in-law, relieved at the ease of their encounter and at how much had been discussed already; and especially pleased with his wife, who had facilitated the evening by insisting that everything be very informal.

'Such an obliging girl, my Mary – never thought we would rub along so comfortably! Very convenient this institution, Crawford, you really must try it sometime. There must be a suitable girl some-where around here' – looking around, as if a likely candidate could have been hidden in the fireplace or behind the curtains. Fanny kept her eyes fixed resolutely on the births and marriages column, so she could not have known how Henry looked in response to this sally, but she heard him say:

'I wonder whether you can appreciate how delicious it is to hear a bachelor of your calibre vaunt the joys of matrimony? But certainly, my dear fellow, when such as yourself show the way, what can the rest of us do but follow?'

His sister was saying something as she closed the piano, to the effect that his false modesty deceived no one, in the face of his reputation as a philanderer. Fanny wondered whether her present state of confusion would persist throughout the evening, and in truth shortly after-wards it seemed to be doing so, for Henry had moved to her side, and she stared at him blankly for some moments before realising that he merely wished to offer her his arm into the dining-room.

Though certainly informal, their meal was copious, and when Fanny compared it with the quiet evenings spent with Lady Bertram and Susan, she could not but admit that a certain measure of elegance and liveliness had its charm. After two hours of her aunt's comments and complaints, Fanny was usually glad to seek the solace of her room and a book. Here, as she sat listening to the latest gossip on the political front, to a review of the newest publications and entertainment, and to some of Henry's adventures in India, she realised that what she considered as her quiet existence at Mansfield was in reality often quite dull.

Whether it was gossip about the Shelley household in Italy, where Mary had been a guest, and had twice met the scandalous Lord Byron, or some inside information about the delegations to Verona and the real reasons for Castlereagh's suicide, it was a style of conversation that Fanny had not often experienced before, even during her marriage, and it threw some light over Tom's relationship with his wife.

The meal was almost over, when her neighbour leaned towards her low-voiced:

'You say very little. Were you bored with my Indian stories?'

'Oh no, I have never heard anyone speak of the place who had so recently returned from it. In fact, I have never met anyone who had actually lived there. Was it true, your description of the dinner-party at the Delhi Residency, with the "nautch" – I think you called it?'

'It means "dance", and that's really all it was. Living at Mansfield, no wonder you found it hard to credit – but I assure you that it happened like that.' There was a small pause, during which Fanny was busy thinking of something to say.

'Had you much difficulty adjusting to life there – I mean at first?'

He reflected a moment and his eyes were sombre: 'There was some, at first. But I was thirsty for action, and reckless enough to volunteer for the most daring expeditions, such as the one to Haryana, so that promotion came fast ... And then' – here there was a slight smile – 'in some ways society there is organised to afford the greatest comfort and luxury to the new recruit from England.'

Here Mary interrupted: 'Oh yes, we can well imagine that! Do tell us more about the native palaces and all the wonderful things you saw.'

But her brother seemed to have changed mood. As they left the dining-room, he turned the conversation aside: 'Actually, in my first four years out there, I did not have more than a half-year's leave taken altogether, so that I simply did not have the opportunity to see very much of the country. Conditions were quite difficult, particularly in Mehwat, most of the time.'

Tom interrupted: 'Did you never have a holiday somewhere?'

'In fact it was impossible to get away for years, though Simpson and myself did manage a sketching holiday in Egypt in '16. We had planned to go on to Athens, but were recalled to deal with some more trouble.' Despite Tom's eager questions, he could not be brought to say more, but turned to his sister for some music: 'For I heard you trying out something delicious just before supper, as we came in.'

Mary moved obligingly to the piano, and as the sentimental melody filled the room, her brother sat staring before him, waving aside tea and coffee, his glass of port ignored beside him, as silent and introspective now as his partner at table had been earlier. Tom had picked up the newspaper, so that Fanny had nothing to do, in the absence of a sewing-basket, but to sit very still in the deep shadow of her winged chair and try to collect her thoughts.

Later, in the warm comfort of her bed before she fell asleep, her mind once again ran over the strange interlude, when she and Henry had sat silently in their armchairs, while Mary continued at the piano and her husband dozed over his newspaper. From where she sat she could see him clearly, though the candle-light did not permit of close observation, and at one point she found herself staring at him, trying to recognise the man she had known. Years of a military existence had given him a stronger and more assured presence, although his face wore the same burnt, fagged look her uncle had worn on his first return from Antigua. Henry's dark hair showed some streaks of grey, and she found herself wondering whether he had not taken a tropical fever of some sort, for at one point it had seemed that the hand that eventually raised the port glass to his lips trembled slightly, and did she imagine that the eye of interrogation turned upon her when this happened glittered feverishly?

Had he intended to speak to her in that moment? He had leaned forward and looked at her intently, and his mouth had moved as in a prelude to speech. Then he seemed to change his mind, had leaned backwards in his armchair and stretched out his legs, his look meditative, as though fixed on a place far removed from the present. Fanny had cast her eyes about the room in search of a distraction, but they fell first upon Mary, by now in the throes of her sonata, and then travelled to her cousin. Tom's hands were folded across his newspaper and his head had fallen backwards in a listening position, which would have been more convincing had his eyes been open and had he not been snoring softly. No help from that quarter, Fanny thought.

She had decided to put a stop to these nonsensical reflections, to rise from her chair at the close of the sonata and plead a diplomatic headache, but was forestalled by the host himself. He graciously dismissed the company, pleading an early start next morning, when everyone was convened to a tour of the estate before breakfast.

7

*F*anny had obviously been included in the early morning ride, and had offered her excuses, for she could as easily imagine herself taking off in a hot-air balloon as setting off on a morning ride with three such equestrian companions, on one of Henry's high-fed horses.

Having promised herself the luxury of a late rising, she was none too pleased to find herself awake very early, and even listening for the sounds of departure from the front steps, which she had ascertained were beneath her window when she rose and drew back the heavy curtains. From where she stood at the window she could now see part of the expanse of ground that rolled down towards the river, and beyond that the autumn woods of Everingham, already golden in the early sunshine.

The beauty of the natural setting accorded perfectly with the harmonious style and the general layout of the house. From a variety of reasons, she had not been able to observe very much last night, but she could now recall their drive up to it in the twilight, and the disposition of some of the major rooms they had seen later. Smaller than Mansfield, it gave an impression of greater airiness and space, probably due to the unified architectural style, for the building was modern, and as yet few additions and modifications had been made. The furnishings of the drawing-room and of the dining-room, which she had admired last night, united taste with style – though she had noticed several pieces of furniture which were obvious relics of an earlier period, they were placed so as to harmonise with the overall décor. Her room, though unusually large and elegant, even by Mansfield standards, was in the main so thoughtfully disposed, with so many pleasant touches, that the overall impression was one of homely comfort.

Fanny stood there at the window half dreaming, till a pebble at the casement made her look down at Mary, standing beside her brother. They were waiting for Tom, whose voice she heard from the doorway below, before he walked out to join them. They turned to where the horses were attended, but not before Mary waved and blew a kiss to the window. Fanny drew back quickly, suddenly conscious of her tumbled hair, and of a quickened heart-beat. Who had thrown the pebble? Had he seen her? He had not seemed to look in her direction, but she could not be sure.

She pulled herself up sharply and decided on an early breakfast, before the others returned. She would spend the rest of the morning in her room with a book, and for the last few hours of her stay at this house would avoid every occasion of private conversation with its master.

Unfortunately for her, the others returned early from their morning ride, and she spent almost half an hour seated in the breakfast-parlour with her host – awaiting the appearance of Mary, while Tom perused the newspapers. She would have wished above all to chat unconcernedly with him, but his unaccustomed silence disconcerted her, as did the way she found him looking at her every time she glanced in his direction. It was a look that did not betray much interest or awareness, but was rather the reflective far-away gaze of the previous evening, as though his mind was fixed on other things, and could have been attributed as much to absent-mindedness as to any other cause.

Immediately after breakfast Tom and Henry disappeared once more with the estimable Barton, and Fanny's comfort was increased, and her early-morning decision facilitated by the fact that Tom returned alone to lunch, bearing the excuses of his brother-in-law, who had been detained by an urgent problem on a homestead nearly two miles away. He had made all the arrangements for their departure, and hoped to see them soon in Town etc. Fanny felt that she had no part in any of these messages, and should have felt more relief at the prospect of a timely departure from Everingham and an early arrival at Mansfield that evening.

This proved to be the case.

The travellers were welcomed back as though they had been

absent for a fortnight. Edmund came running down the drive, as intent on greeting aunt Mary as he was his mother, followed by Susan, and Lady Bertram walked from her sofa to the door of the salon to smile and speak her welcome to her favourite daughter-in-law.

Fanny was disproportionately glad to be home, and safe. She had the impression that the trip had lasted far longer than thirty hours, and she embraced Edmund fondly and clung to him in a small fever of maternal solicitude. She put him to bed herself that night, and as she listened to his childish thanks for her safe return, she felt a strong upwelling of love for him, and a renewed sense of responsibility for this life at her charge. She felt she could never abandon him – for what, she did not inquire of herself. But her dreams that night were unquiet, with half-understood visions and sounds. She seemed at one point to be flying over a moonlit countryside, and later seemed to float in ice-cold water, adrift under a waterfall. Awakened from disturbed sleep to hear the clock ticking in the silent house, she lit a candle and read till her eyes burned and she found sleep at last.

★★★

As is the case on so many days of departure, the next day dawned fair and unseasonably warm. Fanny spent most of the morning in Mary's company, and although she was obliged to share several confidences concerning the lady's husband and mother-in-law, she heard nothing from Mary about her brother, though she knew that he was engaged to meet his sister in London very shortly. The last repast was eaten, the boxes strapped to the coach, the last lost jewellery-box located, the last speeches made, and Edmund had his chance of offering Mary one of his drawings. Mary bid her farewells warmly, plainly delighted to be off at last, though seemingly sincere in her assurances of returning to Mansfield for Christmas. Julia had written a long letter to her new sister-in-law, full of her satisfaction at their connection, and Mary had carelessly shown this missive to Fanny during one of their conversations. Julia and her family were to spend Christmas at Mansfield, to which she looked forward with great pleasure, not the least of which was to renew acquaintance with her dear Mary. She had also written to Fanny, which letter

Fanny sat down to read after the departure of the visitors.

She had only met Julia three times in the past thirteen years. Her first stay at Mansfield, shortly after her marriage, had been a short one – the house had been silent at the time, and Sir Thomas too stern for warmth and hospitality. Three years later, in the summer of 1813, the Yateses had visited once more, this time to present their daughter to her grandparents. This visit Fanny could remember as having been a very long one, for they had arrived shortly after her lying-in for Edmund, and were still in the house when Sir Thomas hastily departed a second time for Antigua. Julia and her child had stayed on after the Hon. John returned to Bath, and were close to their scheduled time of departure when news of the disastrous hurricane reached England. Fanny felt that the presence of her remaining daughter had materially helped in the recovery of Lady Bertram, and they had corresponded sporadically in the intervening years. But life in Bath was either too engrossing, or their budget was too tight to permit of frequent travelling, for Julia had only made one other visit – to bid farewell to her brother. She had been staying with friends in London for the season, and had reached Mansfield just in time to see Edmund, and give some comfort to her mother and to Fanny in the following days. Although their relationship could not be described as close, Fanny thought of her with some kindness, and was pleased to receive her news.

Julia's letter started out with a paragraph dedicated to the pecuniary difficulties inherent in life in Bath, where one was expected to mix in society and entertain in style, especially with the approach of winter. There was a good deal more about winter fashions, before the family's Christmas visit to Mansfield was again confirmed, Fanny thought with as much a view to retrenchment as for any other reason.

The tone of the letter changed in the third paragraph:

I have this instant received your letter with the Great News. Oh, Fanny, imagine how insensitive – they are actually to pay a bride-visit! Not knowing or caring how awkward it will be for everyone, but especially for you – though I suppose there is nothing to be done, in the circumstances! I know my mother has almost no memory these days, and Tom never cared about what anyone thought about anything

– but as Edmund's widow they should have considered your feelings in this case. And – God forbid – is the brother to visit as well? To be sure, what a pleasant family party we shall be at Christmas!

She ended hurriedly, begging for an instant reply and many more details. There was a postscript:

My mother's letter has just arrived – she says she will not receive them at Mansfield – has someone thought to tell her that, if anything, the shoe is on the other foot?

Fanny sat over this letter for some time. Julia's hypocrisy (or something approaching it, in view of her letter to Mary) was not the only thing about it that disturbed her. She was surprised to discover that the somewhat similar sentiments that she had formulated to herself some weeks ago now seemed disagreeable and tiresome, not to mention downright uncharitable.

It occurred to her that there were times when the negative quality of moral insensitivity could be viewed as a social necessity. Obtuse people, however irritating, were also convenient ones to know in certain circumstances, for civilised social intercourse would be impossible were society composed mainly of sensitive souls and high sticklers. A certain degree of blindness to the faults of others seemed in many cases a more attractive quality than the virtue of Christian forgiveness, and the proverbial dogs had never seemed more tolerable than when fast asleep in one's thoughts.

The next day brought Fanny two more letters, the first one from her mother in Portsmouth. The tone of her mother's letter differed considerably from that of Julia's, for she gave only minor importance to the news of Tom's marriage; relegating it to three lines in the final paragraph. Her letter accorded with Julia's, however, in reports of financial embarrassment.

She opened with a list of complaints about the rising costs of living, it seemed she did not know for how long more she would be able to afford to pay rent, food, fuel and Rebecca's salary. She rejoiced that her good husband was lying under the ground insensible to the straits his wife was reduced to. Here Fanny could not avoid a slight shrug as she read, remembering from her single visit to Portsmouth that her father was in a generally insensible state each day after mid-morning, and feeling that his demise from drink some years ago had probably been a blessing in disguise for his family. Mrs Price mentioned that William had written to her some two months ago and sent a handsome donation towards the house-keeping, which sum was now nearly exhausted and she did not know which direction to look for relief. Fanny made a mental note to send her twenty pounds by return post, which she hoped would solve the most pressing problems; wondering once more to herself why her mother, the least managing and most spendthrift of three sisters, should have elected to marry the poorest man.

Her mother's second source of complaint was loneliness, for with John a bailiff on the Bertram estate in Antigua, Sam and Charles both at sea, and with Tom in London articled to a lawyer, since Richard's death from typhoid five years ago she had lived alone in the house with Betsey, who at seventeen was probably harder to control than Fanny could remember her being at five. In addition, it seemed she was grown very comely, and gentlemen-callers had regularly to be repulsed, whether at the door or in the street. Fanny sighed at this last bit of news, regretting once more that she could do nothing for her family beyond the occasional gift of money made out of her personal economies. Although she was not yet apprehensive that Betsey would come upon the town, it was certain that the girl's beauty combined with her mother's lack of both money and wit boded no good for her future.

Rebecca was the third source of dissatisfaction. The years had not improved either her performance or her temperament; and by her mistress' account she was grown as deaf as a doorpost, though seriously courting the butcher's assistant, and therefore unlikely to be in her present position the following spring. Fanny sighed once more. Unsatisfactory as this handmaiden had been, she had stayed with her mother for fourteen years, and her place would not be easily filled on what Mrs Price could afford to pay.

Finally, Mrs Price sent greetings to her sister Lady Bertram,

'whom I am sure has troubles enough of her own, with the unwise marriage of your eldest cousin. These Crawfords have been nothing but trouble from start to finish, though I am sure I cannot see why you would not marry Henry when you could, and avoid a heap of problems'.

Here Fanny could not help smiling at the similarity of thought, if not of language, between her mother and the defunct aunt Norris, who had always held Fanny responsible for Maria's elopement, through her refusal to marry Henry.

Her mother ended by advising Fanny to look out for a husband for Susan. On that point at least, Fanny thought, things were in a fair train. Folding the letter, Fanny reflected that in all the years of her correspondence with her mother since her marriage, she had never yet received a letter that was other than a thinly disguised application for money.

Having already noted with pleasure that her second letter was addressed in William's hand, Fanny was about to open it, when Edmund entered the room. He needed his mother to come with him for a drive about the estate in the pony-trap, for grandmama was dozing and Susan was busy in the still-room; and Jem had declared that he would not drive young Edmund without the presence of a consenting adult.

Regretting that she had not asked Stephen Tilly to start his visits earlier than next week, Fanny put William's letter into her pocket and accompanied her son outdoors. The air was fresh if somewhat keen, though there was still a fair deal of sunshine, and it was delightful to observe the tones of autumn in the trees as they wheeled about the grounds. The joy of Edmund in his mother's company was manifest in his loud singing and whistling, and in the barrage of questions, from the mundane to the philosophical, that he fired at his parent without pausing either for response or breath. Despite being quickly fagged by her offspring, Fanny was very glad that she had made the small gesture to please the little boy, and they returned to the house in high spirits, much satisfied with each other.

The letter, however, lay forgotten in her pocket until she went upstairs to her dressing-room to prepare for dinner, when she sat for more than half an hour poring over it contents.

Naval Headquarters,
Gibraltar, 22 Sept.

My dear Fanny,
 Wonderful as it always is to get one of your letters, with news of everyone at home and at Mansfield, yr. last brought such surprising

news that I find myself replying the very next day, instead of waiting my usual week at least.

The newly-weds must by now be on their wedding-visit at Mansfield. I hope that this has not created more stress than the minimum, and that it has not needlessly complicated your everyday life. You should ,in any case, have thought of an independent establishment before now, and to that end this may be as good a time as any. You are still a young woman, and as Jane observed to me once, Mansfield is not the ideal location for meeting new people, which is what you should do. I can tell you straight – old Thwaite will not do!

But how strange life is! That is what I have been thinking of incessantly since reading your letter. Fanny, shall I tell you something? This is in the strictest confidence, mind you, for I should not want the slightest wind of it to reach my dearest Jane, who has been everything to me for the past eight years. I don't know how far it would surprise you to learn that during my stay at Mansfield all those years ago (before I got my commission) I considered myself very much in love with Mary Crawford.

It was my first acquaintance, at nineteen, with someone from her world, and I was dazzled by her brilliance and charm. For many weeks, I awoke every morning in the anticipation of her smile, and slept every night with the sound of her voice in my ears. I could see how things stood between her and Edmund (and I could also see how it stuck in your throat at the time!) and knew my case to be a hopeless one. Of course, I never dared to speak to her, but I think she knew – there was something in her glance and tone of voice, and she seemed unduly conscious when we danced at your coming-out ball – the only time we ever danced!

How foolish I sound! But when one is a callow youth one's feelings for a woman like her are as a fever in the blood – it takes time to dissipate and resolve itself – in my case it was over a year before I could think of her with indifference. I can even remember the occasion – it was when her name was mentioned one day at table by a senior officer, though I knew by then that she could not marry Edmund, nor you Henry. This I sincerely regretted, for at the time how could I help thinking of him as the best of men? And the truth is, that in despite of all that followed, I still regret his acquaintance. He is the sort of man that is best appreciated by other men, he seems unfortunate in his relations with women. You mentioned his engagement, I sincerely wish him very happy.

I can see now that Tom is in many ways the ideal husband for Mary, and hope that their union will be a long and happy one.

Jane and the children are well and send you affectionate greetings. The summer was intolerably hot, as usual, but now that we have fresher breezes and chilly evenings everyone is more comfortable, including poor Thomas, who is recovering from the measles, and like his older sister asking to be remembered to aunt Fanny and cousin Edmund. Please tell this last that his uncle has an interesting present preparing against my next home-leave, which we all hope will be next spring.

Till then our united wishes to you and to all at Mansfield,

Yr. affectionate brother,

William.

P.S. I hope our mother has received my last, together with enclosure – the posts here continue to be somewhat dicey at times, and she never acknowledges receipt. When you write to her, tell her that our brothers are doing well, I heard from Charles last week, and had a long letter from John last month.

Jane asks me to thank you for the journal of London fashions.

Fanny sat re-reading this letter till the dinner-bell sounded for the second time. Her mind travelled once more over the memory of that distant summer, and she remembered Mary Crawford's words: 'There is more than one way of our being sisters.'

Yes, indeed!

8

*L*ady Bertram had always been one of those fortunate people who remain in relatively good health without any apparent effort, or sometimes in despite of a systematic abuse of the body systems that is a mystery to the less well-constituted. Ever since her marriage – when she had abandoned effort and movement for a sedentary life-style – she had survived almost forty years of inertia combined with excellent meals, the only surprise being that under this regime she had grown neither unduly fat nor very unhealthy.

She had borne fairly well the ill-health and deaths within her family, and apart from the stroke she had suffered on hearing of the tragedy at Antigua, her illnesses had been mild and speedily banished. It was therefore as much to her own surprise as that of her family that her health finally started to fail. She began by complaining of tiredness and shortness of breath, keeping later mornings than usual, and retiring immediately after dinner, for which she seldom had much appetite. A fortnight of this behaviour convinced Fanny that more expert advice than that available from Mr Comyn was necessary, and a summons was sent to London to request the attendance of Sir Edward Lyttleton, an august personage who gravitated about the Court itself, and whose reputation was as immense as the size of his fees.

The great man arrived by coach from London a week later, to spend a night at Mansfield, observe his patient, advise on treatment, rest his horses, eat an excellent dinner, and generally earn his fee. He graciously consulted with Mr Comyn, the two finally agreeing on a regime that while it preserved quiet and rest, would introduce some regular form of gentle exercise. The most obvious would be a daily walk, taken about the grounds of the Park, though the present season was certainly not the best one for such activity. Sharp winds and driving rain are not usually an appropriate accompaniment to healthful exercise. Somewhat unexpectedly, however, Fanny saw that on most days her aunt managed to find half an hour for her daily walk, and even to manifest some pleasure in the effort, though her years of lolling on her sofa had ill-prepared her for the very real satisfaction of a brisk autumn walk amid falling leaves. Her appetite improved, as did her sleep and general outlook.

By early November she had already been exercising regularly for over a fortnight, and had taken the habit of walking in the early afternoon, when there was the best expectation of an autumn sunshine. Her usual companion was young Edmund, who sincerely appreciated the company of his grandmother, if not of her appendage, Pug – who was grown more snappish as a result of this untoward activity. On the days when Stephen Tilly attended Edmund at the house, this walk had been incorporated into their programme, and Fanny was not unduly surprised at the frequency with which Susan found it necessary to make one of the party as well.

Edmund was already showing signs of improved knowledge and wisdom as a result of Mr Tilly's attentions. With his time more actively occupied, he was rapidly learning the common skills for a boy of his age, and seemed much happier as a result. Fanny was reflecting on this one afternoon in her room while attending to some small household tasks, and her mood was both thankful and complacent. She had watched the departure of the daily cortège from her window, and reckoned on at least forty minutes of peace to complete what needed to be done.

So much greater was her surprise to be interrupted barely fifteen minutes later by a breathless, white-faced Susan, who called out to her to 'come immediately, for something terrible has happened. Our aunt – she seemed to fall suddenly, and lay like a stone – oh, Fanny, could it be another stroke, or worse?'

Fanny was already on her feet and at the door, and heard some of this on the way to her aunt's boudoir, whence it seemed that Stephen had already carried her, leaving Edmund to return to the house with Pug, as best he could. In a few moments Fanny and Susan were beside her, to find their most serious apprehensions upheld: it appeared to be another stroke.

Stephen had already left to fetch Mr Comyn, and Fanny thought it wise to send at once to Tom in London, as well as to Sir Edward, requesting another urgent visit. Upon her return to the sick-room, she could see that her aunt was still motionless, and sat beside her for almost an hour, in great distress, only attempting to caress her hands and talk to her gently. At last Mr Comyn arrived, confirmed the diagnosis, and started preparations for bleeding the patient. This seemed to take very slow effect, as did the hot and cold compresses that followed, for it was yet another hour before her ladyship opened her eyes and showed some signs of awareness.

She was unable to speak or make any movement, though by her facial expression she manifested such concern when the supper-bell went, that they immediately decided that one of them would stay beside her at all times. It was necessary to take shifts to accomplish this, and Fanny thought it expedient to invite Stephen Tilly to move to Mansfield for the time being, as well as to consult with Mr Comyn on the choice of a nurse, who could undertake the heavier tasks involved in the care of the sick woman.

The next morning saw the arrival of this lady. Heavy, glowering and short of speech, Abigail Smith was at first sight very far removed from the image of a ministering angel, but she seemed conscientious in her execution of Mr Comyn's orders, and by the time she arrived both Fanny and Susan were in such a need of rest as would have induced them to accept an even less prepossessing handmaiden.

Lady Bertram had not spoken as yet, but she had passed a relatively peaceful night, and was able to smile at Edmund when he brought Pug to see her in the morning. Sir Edward was expected either that evening or the following day, since it transpired he was visiting a friend in the same county, but Fanny was in an optimistic mood from these events, long before he arrived.

He ordered the cessation of all attempts at bleeding, concentrating instead on the administration of cordials designed to stimulate the function of the heart. It was another two days before he pronounced the patient out of immediate danger, though she faced several weeks of careful nursing before any resumption of normal activity could be envisaged. Lady Bertram was still largely immobile, and had only partially recovered her speech, but Fanny in great thankfulness bade farewell to Sir Edward the next day, followed within the week by the taciturn Mrs Smith, who had been discovered getting at the contents of the wine-cupboard one afternoon, while her charge was asleep.

This left the essential duties of nursing their aunt to fall squarely upon Fanny and Susan, aided in the heavier tasks by whichever members of the household could be best spared from their duties, or more often by Stephen Tilly. This last continued as a guest in the house, though Fanny often considered how unfair it was to use the term, when she saw how untiringly he worked at the more arduous aspects of nursing, and at the same time kept Edmund occupied for several hours a day at lessons and at what might be termed leisure-activities.

At this time, Fanny came increasingly to like and to respect the young man. His calm good humour and unfailing support were what she grew to rely upon, and she saw in the small gestures and looks of Lady Bertram that their patient had the same reliance on him, in fact it soon became difficult to distinguish between the warmth of the welcome accorded to Edmund and to Edmund's tutor. By the time Lady Bertram was able to say a complete sentence and take her first halting steps across the room, Fanny would have been prepared to witness to anyone, that if it came to a match between Stephen and her sister, the advantage would go largely to Susan.

This is not to say that she undervalued in any way the good qualities of her favourite sister. On the contrary – Susan's strength, her energy, patience and good nature, were invaluable attributes in the sick-room, and Lady Bertram grew increasingly dependent upon her as well as upon Stephen. It was her greatest pleasure to have them both about her, the invisible current of sympathy that was tangible between the two young people seemed to exert a beneficent effect upon her as well. However, she still preferred to turn to Fanny for advice when faced with one of the minor problems that loom large in the mind of a convalescent. Thus, a decision on which shawl to wear to dinner, or whether or not to allow her maid to wash her hair, had always to be referred to Fanny, adding to the other duties that were fagging her.

The month of November dragged on slowly. Fanny thought that she had never been so tired before for any prolonged period of her life, certainly she had never spent as many wakeful nights. Her aunt was not really a bad patient – she was rarely fearful and only occasionally querulous – but Fanny was sometimes almost overcome by the sheer monotony of the sick-room, of its unvarying routine, and the minutiae of its regulations.

Added to her physical tiredness there was an increasing nagging worry about Edmund. Although Stephen (she thought of him under no other name by this time) was spending several hours with him every morning, and more time again every afternoon, she felt that she herself was unable to see her son often enough, and was in danger of losing track of his development. She rarely had the time to supervise any of his meals, games or bedtime, and had noted with a pang how easily he turned to Stephen with a question or a problem.

Sitting up in bed one morning in late November, after a night in which she had only managed to snatch four hours of sleep, she decided to put aside some time each day to spend with Edmund, before turning to read a letter placed on her tray. Her immediate assumption was that it was from Tom, who had not yet acknowledged receipt of her communication about his mother, though she had sent him two other messages since.

A glance at the envelope revealed that this letter was from William, and she turned it over slowly, examining the address and the date, savouring the moment of reading. It had been written and posted on the third day of November, and was obviously penned in a great hurry, by one who had a thousand pressing details to attend to.

He had some good news to announce – he was within hours of departing for England, and would probably be in sight of its shores by the time she read this letter – in fact, there was a distinct possibility that he would arrive before it. His leave had perforce been anticipated by several months, as he had been detailed to accompany Vice Admiral Heywood to England for discussions with the War Office. He hoped to see his sister, even if only for a few days, sometime at the end of the year; though this was by no means certain, as he must necessarily be in London for the first four to five weeks. Old Heywood was known for a crusty old b——, and he doubted he would be able to get away in time for any Christmas festivity anywhere, though he planned to try and see his mother in

Portsmouth as soon as he could, if possible on his way to London. The main disadvantage of this sudden change of plan was that he would be separated from his dear Jane and the children at this season of the year, which they would spend busily packing their boxes, though they would be lucky to get away before the end of January. He had great hopes of securing a safe berth in an English port for at least a year, but if that did not succeed and he was obliged to return overseas, it was no great matter, and he remained her affectionate brother, William.

9

*F*anny read this letter with a mixture of feelings, her lids drooping as she read, and twice having to go back and read a sentence over again to grasp its meaning. Her main sensation was the great joy of knowing that William was perhaps already in England, and that she was certain to see him sometime soon. If only she could take the stage-coach to London and seek him out! Not for the first time, she regretted that she could not leave Mansfield whenever she wished – its very comfort and charm operated as a cocoon against the world outside.

Then she recollected that even were she free to roam about the country at will, she could not leave her aunt at present. She had made a remarkably rapid recovery, and was currently moving about slowly aided only by a walking-stick. Her speech – albeit somewhat slow and slurred – had returned, and she was making plans for resuming her regular daily walks after the New Year; still, she could not be left alone in the house at this time.

Mrs Manners and her staff were well-trained and efficient, and Susan shared in some of the daily organisation of the house, but she could not be expected to act as chatelaine. Fanny knew that the present state of affairs, when Mansfield was really without a mistress, could not last much longer.

It was time for Tom and his wife to take their obligations seriously and decide on a more permanent residence, or else increase the responsibilities of the estate-manager, and shut up the house for the greater part of the year. Lady Bertram and her two nieces could be settled in London or possibly in Huntingdon, where an ancient aunt – whom she visited regularly – kept a large house eventually destined for her. The dower house on the estate, currently in very poor condition, could be restored for them, or they could even use the little cottage in the village (known as the White House and last occupied by Mrs Norris), which was lying vacant. This would not be an easy decision to make, resulting in certain inconvenience and some resentment in every case, but Fanny could not see how Tom could continue to sidestep his duties.

She was somewhat concerned at not having heard from either him or Mary after she had contacted them about Lady Bertram's illness, more than a fortnight ago. All that she had received so far was a formal note from Tom's agent in London – they were currently visiting friends in Richmond, had been informed of the problem, and would communicate with her shortly.

The next day brought letters from both of them. Tom's communication was typically brief: he was very concerned at the news about his mother, but it was practically impossible to leave London at this moment. He counted on Fanny for regular reports and had notified his bankers to supply her with any supplementary funds she might require. Mary was keeping well, and was writing to her by the same post.

Mary's letter was much longer, the first part evidently having been written before they received the news from Mansfield:

Russell Square, 7 Nov.

My dear Fanny,

You should have accepted my invitation to return here with us! The season is only just starting, but already you would feel the difference between life here and the existence at Mansfield. We have been out to dinner twice this week, to the theatre once, and to a vocal concert at the Rooms with that fat Italian woman – I had to leave early, feeling very unwell not just from her singing, but from a cause that you have guessed already – we expect an increase of the Bertram family in the summer! Tom is absolutely delighted, and as for me? Let me say that for the moment I am content to be spoiled by everyone, and am somewhat resigned to the experience, though actively looking out for an excellent nurse. I am ill most mornings, and very often in the evenings as well. I feel quite strongly that if this is woman's work I want no more of it. Tom shall have his héritier, and after that we shall see.

Do spread the news around at Mansfield in the appropriate quarters, so that belle-maman *and the others will not expect too much of me at Christmas. I shall of course need to consult my personal physician before leaving London.*

I am very pleased with the house here, it is well-situated and designed, and both spacious and elegant. Henry has been helping me with planning the re-furnishing, we have completed our designs on paper for the drawing-room and reception-rooms, and move on to the bedrooms next week. As you can imagine, the kitchens are none of my affair, particularly at this time, when I cannot bear the sight or smell of food.

Henry thinks that when complete, our efforts will almost double the value of the property, so it will be time well-spent. He has retained his rooms, though he spends a great deal of time with us. I am a little surprised by the fact that he does not accompany us everywhere. He has only been out with us once since he arrived last week, and that to the theatre. It was quite amusing to see the reception he got! All my friends, their daughters' nieces or whatever, had to find an excuse for dropping into our box and trying for a conversation with him, though the 'Moor of Venice' himself never scowled as convincingly as my brother, for most of the evening.

I find him somewhat changed, for he does not rattle on as he used to do, neither flirt as outrageously as was his wont – no more than the strictest minimum, I assure you. He is grown almost dull – one would think him already married.

But that has not kept some of my friends away, au contraire! *Jean Nevers seems to be dying for him – she bombards him daily with letters and invitations, and I have had reports of her lying in wait for him in the Park, on afternoons. Madelon D'Albrecht from the Embassy, who is one of my dearest friends, and is saddled with an ancient husband, told me yesterday that he could have her on a salver if she wished – she was certain her husband would not notice, or mind if he did!*

It has always been thus with Henry – once, many years ago, he told me that he regretted this effect he had on some women – though I noticed that he used it to suit his own ends on some occasions! But now he seems bored, not amused. He is less pleasant company than he used to be, and spends hours locked in his room smoking that horrible 'hookah' of his, or out riding accompanied by none but his native bearer, with whom he seems most at ease.

I think he has a sort of recurring fever — of the type they have in southern Italy — for I have seen several packets and vials among his things. I shall try to get him to consult with Sir Edward; he can afford none but the best now that he is returned so rich. This could of course be one of the reasons for his present popularity, though not many people outside our immediate circle know of the immense fortune it seems he amassed in India. I suspect this was the reason for his cancelled engagement in May. Perhaps he got to thinking that young (too young?) Lisa Seton was after his wealth — or had she rather discovered the existence of his native mistress? I know from something he mentioned that he had to pay off both of them, handsomely, before leaving Delhi!

Why am I telling you all this? Is it because I am alone at home today, and not feeling sick for the first time in days? Or is it rather because you are one of the few women of my acquaintance who is not preoccupied with Henry, though he once loved you sincerely, and you — what were your feelings for him all those years ago? Or were we both in love with the same man? This is an idea that has only come to me recently — how drôle!

But enough of my brother, and here is some news of yours. At dinner last evening I had it from Admiral Telford's wife that their dear friend Heywood is expected at the War Office any day now, and is to be accompanied by a certain interesting Captain Price! We are bound to meet at some Admiralty receptions and suppers — don't worry, I shall keep you informed.

Tomorrow we leave for a few days at Richmond with Flora Stornaway, whom you may remember, though she has been widowed for the past five years. She has aged amazingly, and grown correspondingly bitter. I felt sorry for her when we met at dinner last week, for she begged us to visit her 'for old times' sake'. We shall spend the end of the week with her, and then find an excuse to return, as we shall need several days of preparation for our first large reception which will be on the 23rd. I do wish you could be here, I have already received over sixty acceptances!

12 Nov. Written in great haste — we have just arrived in Russell Square. Got your message yesterday — it seems there was some delay in transmission. We are very sorry indeed at the news about bellémère (Fanny, do I detect a sly smile? I have no serious reason to wish for her disparition, for the moment anyway) — and I have arranged with Tom's bankers to release to you any funds that you may need. Do keep us informed of her progress, especially as to what Sir Edward thinks, he is particularly reputable. We shall try to push forward our date for Mansfield, though hoping that in the meanwhile the worst will not occur — I have scarcely anything convenable in black!

Fondest wishes etc.

Mary Bertram.

Fanny sat contemplating this missive for a long time, unaware of the gathering dusk outside the windows, till a maid entered to light the candles, and tell her that Master Edmund had been asking for her during his supper. She replied hastily, before returning to her reading, once more overcome by the same mixture of incomprehension and revulsion that had always affected her in the past on reading one of Mary's letters, or after any serious conversation with her. She had always found her cynicism hard to understand, and her particular form of wit heartless, but this letter revealed something more: Mary's letters had usually reflected her thinking to a far greater degree than was possible with her sophisticated style of conversation, but they were more amusing than intimate. Here for the first time she seemed to feel a need to confide and to communicate, especially on the subject of her brother, before lapsing into her usual vein in the concluding paragraph.

Fanny would have liked to spend some moments reflecting on certain passages of this letter, particularly on those pertaining to Henry, but here she was caught for time, for clearly she had to hasten to Edmund's bed-time ceremony, and then spend the rest of the evening attending her aunt at supper and to bed. Lady Bertram no longer needed the heavy drugged sleep of the very ill, but in consequence she suffered from insomnia, and Fanny or Susan not infrequently spent several hours at night reading to her, and generally attending to her needs. Folding the letter, she regretted that she had not received it at breakfast, for now there was no opportunity to reply immediately. It was enough for the moment to know that neither Tom nor his wife could be counted on at Mansfield for at least another fortnight, and that they considered their presence at an elegant soirée in London of more crucial importance than at his mother's bedside in what could have been a terminal illness.

It was necessary to present Lady Bertram with the information Mary had given her about her condition, and to put forward the coming event as the main reason why she could not travel at the moment. Fanny sat thinking this over the next morning at breakfast, and sighed as she prepared for a session of half-truths and lies, wishing in vain that this sad task did not fall so frequently to her lot. She remembered this feeling again in the late morning, as she sat in the drawing-room listening to Dr Thwaite, and found herself once more in a position where she felt obliged to prevaricate.

He came bearing gifts, some pears and plums from his greenhouse, and a honeycomb from the hive, which he handed over with an unusually bashful air, muttering something about 'sweets to the sweet'. Fanny felt inclined to giggle, but thanked him composedly on behalf of her aunt, who would be well enough for morning visits in another few days. At this the good doctor became somewhat confused, and was apparently trying to say something, but either bashfulness, the tightness of his collar, or some other reason kept him from expressing himself clearly. While he haltingly searched for the words that he needed, Fanny, who had already guessed that the good things were rather intended to cheer the healthy than relieve the sick, thought it best to feign ignorance on this point and change the subject of conversation.

This led them to talk of the absent master of Mansfield and his lady, and here again Fanny saw herself upholding an untruth, albeit from the purest of motives. As she repeated her tale of Mary 'being temporarily incapacitated and hence unable to travel', a sixth sense was warning her of something else.

She remembered a moment last Sunday during the sermon, when a particular passage on the duties of the married state had been stressed with more than one glance in the direction of the family stall, much to the satisfaction of some members of the congregation. Two days ago he had dined at Mansfield — albeit at a reduced table — and she could now recall some mysterious glances and phrases, which in her chronic tiredness she had not registered at the time.

It rather seemed as though the parson of Mansfield was girding up his loins, so to speak, to take the plunge, which she sincerely hoped he would not do. Her feelings were indifferent to him, but she was too gentle to enjoy causing anyone pain, and she considered him too respectable a man to become the butt of public humour.

With real relief, therefore, she heard the subdued commotion of Edmund's approach, with Stephen in tow, come to invite the visitor to join in a pre-luncheon expedition to the lower meadow, where the newest colt was being broken by Jem. Fanny did not await the ceremony of his reply, but took herself off thankfully to relieve Susan. Lady Bertram would soon awake from her morning nap and want to take a turn about the drawing-room, and she thought it probable that Susan herself might feel the need for some of the fresh air of the lower meadow.

10

*I*t was no great surprise to anyone at Mansfield when, in
addition to the other meals they enjoyed in each other's
company, Susan and Stephen Tilly discovered an affinity for
the most appropriate breakfast-hour, and could be encountered
early on most mornings in the breakfast-parlour, eating and
conversing softly, before starting the business of the day.

Fanny did not know how far they were in each other's confidence,
but to the observer it was obvious that besides mutual admiration,
they shared youthful optimism and some common aspirations for
the future. She admired not only their restraint but also their generosity, in spending what was probably a unique period of courtship
at Mansfield, taking care of a sick woman and a little boy. These
thoughts were running through her head as she came downstairs
one morning a week later, and opening the door of the breakfast-
parlour, saw her sister and Stephen seated side by side in what was
obviously a very private conversation.

Feeling an intruder, she stood in the doorway, embarrassed and
undecided whether to retreat or advance, when Stephen suddenly
rose to his feet, and with only an awkward 'Good morning!' to her,
hastily left the room. Fanny looked at Susan with some concern,
before walking over to the table to stand beside her sister. If any
important communication was forthcoming, this was surely the
time for it. But she waited several long seconds in vain, for though
Susan blushed with obvious discomfiture, she remained silent,
finishing her toast and chocolate before speaking:

'Would you mind if I took Edmund out nutting with me this
afternoon? We would use the trap, and take Jem with us. Stephen
needs to visit his uncle on some business.'

She blushed again as she spoke, and Fanny thought it wisest to acquiesce quietly before starting her breakfast. Doubtless the young people knew what they were about, and she relied upon them to tell her their news as soon as there was any to tell. Watching her sister leave the room, Fanny sighed gently, wishing once more that prospects were brighter for this couple. As matters stood, it could be a year or even longer before their means permitted them to marry, assuming both families agreed, and though this delay might be relatively unimportant for Stephen, at almost twenty-eight Susan was of an age when she had really very little time to waste if she planned the founding of a family.

She thought of her mother's pleasure at the prospect of Susan's marriage to a well-connected young clergyman, but she did not know enough of Stephen's background to guess the reaction of his family, for it was certain that Susan was practically penniless. Apart from the small amount that Fanny could spare her from her own inadequate portion, and from her connection to the Mansfield family, she had no settlement to bring a prospective husband – nothing except her excellent health, good humour and common sense. It could be argued that many a fine lady does not do as well in the final analysis, but not everyone may concur.

Were Edmund alive, she would have appealed to him at this juncture, but she did not think it appropriate to ask anything of Tom. It was not that he was mean, but rather that his own ill-judged spending kept him constantly too close to the edge of insolvency for the likelihood of any generous gesture, though his marriage must have alleviated his present position considerably. She guessed that Mary's handsome marriage-portion had cleared his debts and would pay for the planned improvements to the estate as well as the town house, but naturally she had no details, and in any case these would not advance the cause of Susan.

That afternoon, while Lady Bertram dozed in her boudoir, Fanny took an invigorating walk about the grounds of the Park. Apart from a curious jackdaw and the occasional tardy squirrel, she enjoyed the total solitude of its trees, and the brisk little winds that stirred the thick carpet of leaves underfoot. It was a blue winter's day, sunny and fresh, and Fanny found one of her favourite seats – a fallen tree – before taking out for re-reading the letter she had received this morning.

From Tom, it was neither very long nor very informative, though not without interest. He began by congratulating Fanny on his mother's speedy recovery – her reassuring messages had been a great comfort to himself and his dear Mary – and Mary's health was a subject of some concern at the moment. Thoroughly exhausted after the work of presiding at their reception, she now needed rest and recuperation. He thought of advancing their trip to Mansfield by about a week to give her time for this before the inevitable round of visiting began, which he hoped Fanny would do her best to curtail, as in her present fragile state Mary must be spared all excessive effort. There was some more in this vein before he concluded with the news that they had met William twice. He did not seem to have too much time for visiting (though he had attended their reception last Saturday which had been an amazing success!) and was this morning gone out somewhere with Henry. Tom sent every kind thought to his mother especially, and to everyone at Mansfield. Mary had added a footnote to the effect that their party had been the crush of the season, that now she was totally *epuisée*, but had lots of news for her dear Fanny, whom she looked forward to seeing soon.

Fanny was intrigued by the thought of William and Henry out somewhere together, till she recollected the number of acquaintances Henry still had at the Admiralty, and the useful introductions that could yet be made. William had obviously simply taken up with Henry where they had left off – on the best of terms. She deduced that relationships between men were often simpler when there were no women in the case. Then she remembered William's reference to Mary Crawford in one of his recent letters, and wondered how their reunion had gone. She began to be impatient for a letter from William.

Strolling back to the house in the dusk, Fanny planned to repeat this pleasant walk as soon as possible, and the very next day agreed with pleasure to a proposal by Susan to join her and Edmund in their afternoon walk, as Stephen would once more be unavailable. She realised that this second absence must mean something, in a person as regular and conscientious as Stephen, but without any information forthcoming from either of the principals, it was not wise to even hazard a guess.

Lady Bertram heard of the projected walk at luncheon, and showed some signs of wanting to accompany them. In the event, however, it was her deputy, Pug, who went with them, while she dozed comfortably on her sofa. Fanny was relieved. She thought it wiser that her aunt's walks be deferred until she could move without the aid of a walking-stick, and there was now a better chance of Susan talking freely to her, in the absence of another adult.

But this did not happen. Susan talked and laughed a great deal – as much with her nephew as with her sister – and she admonished both Edmund and Pug for loitering, chasing them around trees and down the grassy slope that bordered the ornamental lake. All three looked hot, dirty and happy as they rejoined Fanny to make their way back to the waiting house, but no word of confidence had yet been exchanged between the sisters.

Fanny decided to speak.

'Susan, is there anything you want to tell me – I mean of a purely personal nature – possibly concerning … another person?' She hesitated before continuing: 'You know that I would like to help you if I can – '

Here she broke off, for there seemed nothing more to say until her sister opened the floodgates. Susan was again blushing painfully, and chose her words with caution:

'My dear Fanny, you are too good!' She seized her sister's hand and kissed it affectionately before continuing: 'I promise that you will be the first to know, as soon as there is any news. In the meanwhile … just pray that all goes well – Edmund, *if Pug falls into the lake, I shall send you in to fetch him!*'

And away she sped behind the retreating pair, leaving Fanny feeling considerably relieved, but none the wiser.

In the back courtyard they met Mr Comyn, coming away from visiting his patient. He professed himself very gratified with her progress; he had brought a different sleeping-draught for her, and recommended some slight modifications of diet for the coming weeks. If all went well, she should be well enough, with precaution, to spend a happy Christmas season with the rest of the family. This news was enough to send Edmund whooping up the stairs to the presence of his grandmother with Pug snapping at his heels, and pursued by Susan, who was determined to get him cleaned up for his bed-time.

★★★

The next morning brought Fanny a letter from William in London. It was already a week old, having obviously been carried about in his pocket for several days before posting. Rather brief, it told mainly of his voyage, the problems attendant on his present mission with old Heywood, and the few brief hours of leave he had spent in Portsmouth,with their mother.

> *She seems hale enough, in my opinion, though spinning long yarns about Betsey, who it seems has two or three admirers at least, or was it that I had not the time to stay for all the rest? Seriously though, Fanny, our sister has become a very beautiful girl, in appearance more like a Bertram than a Price – in fact she favours Maria remarkably. I gathered from our parent that she resembles Maria in other ways, being disobedient and wilful, and consequently I took some time to talk to her – came away with the impression that all she wanted really was a change from our mother's company, for which who shall blame her? There was also much about Rebecca and the butcher's assistant, which I shall spare you.*
>
> *London is very full at the moment, though we get no chance of any enjoyment – being in interminable meetings all day and institutionary dinners every evening. I visited Tom two days after my arrival. I was very pleased to meet Henry again, though I would hardly have recognised Mary. Unfortunately unable to accept their many invitations, but I will try to attend their reception on Saturday, if only because I hear two admirals will be on duty!*

For the first time, a letter from William seemed somewhat unsatisfactory to his sister. Fanny had grown increasingly impatient for details of what was happening in London, and she hoped that someday soon William (or even Mary, there being no hope for anything in that nature from Tom) would sit down and write her a long letter, giving her all the smallest details of what was going on. In all her years at Mansfield, she had never before felt the same urgent curiosity about events in the nation's capital.

11

It was now several days since Edmund had obtained the right to keep the young cat Timmy in his room at night, which complicated bed-time for the pair of them, but Fanny insisted on being present at the ceremony, not departing silently till the proper state of drowsiness had been induced in both young creatures, which augured well for a long and quiet night. The next evening, as she silently closed the nursery door and crossed the landing to go to her own room to prepare for the evening, she was handed a hurriedly written note from Stephen, begging for an urgent interview with her. The housemaid informed her that he was waiting for her in the library, and she hurried there, remembering with some disquiet that she had not seen him for almost three days.

He stood awaiting her in the middle of the room, pale and restless in appearance, though not unhappy – much the opposite, it seemed. Wasting no time, they were no sooner seated than he came straight to the point: which was, to request Susan's hand in marriage, and to consult with Fanny as to the most efficient means of obtaining this end.

Fanny did not pretend surprise, but could not help alluding to his somewhat erratic behaviour over the past few days. The whole story then spilled out, as if Stephen was relieved to have the opportunity of confession. It was as follows: two summers ago, when Stephen was down from Oxford for the summer to stay with his uncle, he had encountered the older daughter of Mr Potts, the village shopkeeper. Amy Potts was an amiable girl in addition to being very pretty, and her single aim in life at the time was to find a way of leaving home. Marriage seeming the surest means of achieving this end, she did not hesitate to consider herself in love, and accepted to become secretly engaged after a minimal number of meetings.

Stephen at this point admitted that his feelings ceased to be engaged very early on, but an inappropriate sense of responsibility and manly honour on his side kept their illicit correspondence going for almost a year. It was Amy who at last realised that her young admirer had no immediate prospects of any sort material to her main aim, and initiated the break which had been effectuated by mutual consent last summer. He had not heard from her again, nor even thought of her often, his overwhelming sentiment at the time had been one of relief, strong enough to carry him through the rest of the year till his meeting with Susan this summer.

Fanny kept her smile to herself as she thought how well-regulated this young man was, whose sentiments manifested themselves so conveniently in the summer. She could not help inquiring how it was that the souvenir of Amy had arisen so unseasonably in early winter. Stephen's answer was serious; he had been speaking to his uncle three days ago on the subject of Susan when the name of Amy and their previous correspondence had somehow been raised – it seemed that last year his uncle had not been as totally duped as he hoped. He was of the opinion that Stephen, though no longer engaged, yet bore some moral responsibility towards Amy – he should at least discover her circumstances before proposing marriage to another, especially when the second match was nearly as ill-advised as the first.

Himself anxious by this time that their romantic and somewhat senseless correspondence should not have adversely affected Amy's marital prospects by undermining her sense of reality, Stephen had hurried off to visit her family yesterday, where he learnt of her recent marriage to a local farmer, and obtained her direction, less than two miles away. This very morning he had seen her snugly established and in the way of enlarging her family, and had returned to his uncle's house with the sole purpose of obtaining his approval to an engagement with Susan.

Fanny sensed that this had not been easy. His previous *affaire* could be used to brand Stephen as immature, and though he argued that his relationship with Susan was founded on a firmer basis of friendship and mutual respect, yet he had only known her for five months. Dr Thwaite thought it advisable, in view of the fact that Susan was more than two years older than Stephen, and could perhaps do considerably better for herself in the near future, for them to wait for another year – this with a view to him obtaining a living in the meantime (and, Fanny silently added to herself, to seeing what the Bertrams could do for her).

Stephen was his uncle's heir. Normally, he would have advanced this point with a view to strengthening his position with Fanny during this interview. Instead, he passed it over somewhat rapidly and shamefacedly, which reinforced in Fanny the idea that the good doctor planned a marital adventure himself, in the near future. Knowing as she did the outcome of any such application if it was made to her – as seemed likely – she was the more inclined to settle for an immediate and formal engagement between Susan and Stephen, that their future happiness might not depend on the whims and fancies of any except themselves.

She therefore willingly gave her own approval to the match, promising to write immediately to her mother, and to consult with her brother William as to the possibility of a small eventual settlement on Susan. This was more than Stephen had hoped for, and he earnestly requested permission to speak with Susan immediately. After a further half-hour spent tête-à-tête in the library, the beaming couple entered the supper-room as late and as red-faced as could reassure any observer of the sincerity of their affection.

Susan came to her sister's room that night, bursting with happiness and gratitude, and full of schemes for the future. Fanny felt as happy for Susan as it was possible to feel in the circumstances – lacking only the assurance of the young couple's material welfare. But she could not help catching some of her sister's enthusiasm, for what is mere money to those in possession of their youth, strength and dreams? Watching Susan's shining eyes, and her happy smile as she talked and laughed in the candle-light, describing their plans for a cosy and frugal existence, Fanny could not refrain from giving her a warm sisterly hug before dismissing her to a night of sweet peace and pleasant dreams.

Her own night was not as peaceful – she spent more than an hour after Susan's departure reflecting on her sister's chances of future happiness, which she concluded were well-founded, largely based on the merits of her chosen partner. From there, her mind wandered to her own period of courtship and early married life. True, Edmund and herself had never known material want, and their relationship had been founded on every affectionate feeling, but had it really been a happy marriage? Fanny shocked herself with the question, which had never occurred to her before. She had simply assumed that since they had loved each other sincerely, they must have been happily married.

For the first time, she found herself thinking deeply on the nature and implications of the sentiment labelled as 'love'. For instance, how had her love for Edmund been so radically different from her feelings for William? She had been jealous of Edmund's obvious and immediate attraction to Mary Crawford, and of the strength of the passion he developed for her, which was evidently very different from what he ever felt for his young cousin. Yet, she had felt some jealousy of Jane when William had eventually married, so what did that imply? Long intense moments of introspection gave her an answer, albeit unsatisfactory: she loved William as much as a sister could love a brother, but it was a sentiment that entirely precluded passion or the perspective of marriage, though it could on occasion be possessive. Fanny had considered Edmund as her *other* brother, the only one she *could* marry, and she had married him.

She stopped the effort of thinking for a moment, realising that she was breathing deeply, as though after physical effort. Her mind refused to continue this line of thought, but veered away from herself back to Susan. Her sister's feelings for Stephen now appeared well-balanced, for she had become convinced that a mixture of friendship, affection and passion were necessary ingredients for permanence and stability.

Here Fanny got out of bed somewhat abruptly, and taking her bedside candle to the dressing mirror sat in silence looking at her face in the candle-light. Apart from the dark shadows under her eyes from many nights spent sitting with her aunt, her face looked back at her smooth and untroubled, the sparkling hazel eyes and clear petal skin framed by an abundance of soft brown curls. Fanny did not look like a conventional widow, and she was beginning to realise that she did not feel like one, either. Neither did she feel remotely like a heroine, though this is not pertinent to

72

the issue, for even the least informed reader knows that heroines come in all shapes and sizes. She stared into the clear depths of her own eyes for several minutes, trying to read the secrets of her soul, before returning to her bed and her thoughts.

She forced her mind back to herself and her years with Edmund, and asked herself a very difficult question: had there been any passion in her marriage? Several minutes of painful reflection followed before she admitted a truth to herself: as far as this strong sentiment was concerned, on her side there had been very little, and from Edmund almost none. At eighteen, she had been too innocent, and too fixed on her childhood affection for one who had always been a beloved brother and mentor. Edmund had come to her exhausted and broken by the strength of his passion for Mary, and especially by his deception at the revelation of her true nature. They had both needed peace and emotional security, and Mary was right in her comment that they had taken refuge in each other. They were both horrified by the realisation that he would certainly have married Mary had the scandal not erupted around Henry and Maria. Fanny found herself looking at the ancient scandal from a different angle – for the first time, she realised that it had in fact saved Edmund from a disastrous marriage, one which could even have destroyed him – for he was nothing like his brother. His love for Mary had been a highly idealised sentiment, and would not have long survived any contact with reality.

At this point, she lit a candle and tried to read, but found it impossible to concentrate on the printed words describing some undistinguished travels to the East – neither could she peruse the lithographs of ruined palaces and temple façades with any interest. Her mind kept on returning to the same question: what was the nature and strength of that feeling that had driven a Maria Bertram to throw away her marriage and social position in the hope of persuading Henry Crawford to marry her?

Long moments of reflection on this subject yielded very little. From childhood she had been afraid of strong feeling, her inherent timidity shrank from loud language, strong gestures and other physical manifestations of emotion. Her feelings rather turned inwards – she felt that they were both strong and deep, but invisible. She could not imagine herself in Maria's position, or subject to such passions, even were they reciprocated.

And what had Henry felt for Maria? To the youthful Fanny it had seemed that he was amusing himself at the expense of her cousins, strongly solicited as he was by both of them. She could not, even now, conceive of a mentality in which flirtation was merely a bad habit; instead she asked herself another more crucial question: if the timely scandal had saved Edmund from a disastrous marriage, from what had it saved Fanny Price? She had known, even at the time, that had Edmund married Mary, she would have been driven by her own conscience and rectitude to attempt to overcome her feeling for him by marriage with someone who really loved her – and who could do so much for her family. In retrospect, she saw that she would almost certainly have married Henry Crawford twelve years ago, within months of Edmund's marriage. Here once more she hesitated some time before continuing her self-examination. Would such a marriage have brought her happiness? Of what sort?

Sharp as an arrow the answer lodged in her breast – she would have known what it was to be loved passionately, for herself. She stopped here and tried to close her mind to the pain of knowledge. But there was no escape, and she had to snatch desperately at some things, as though at straws, to save herself from drowning. She reminded herself of Henry's profligacy, of the unlikelihood of his constancy to any woman, of the scenes she had witnessed at Mansfield – especially during the theatricals – and of the references in Mary's letter, particularly to his native mistress in Delhi. She forced herself to concentrate on these as strongly as she could, till with the first grey dawnlight she ceased turning on the pillow and fell into a troubled sleep.

Heavy-eyed at breakfast next morning, Fanny had yet several small but pressing problems to solve, and these were not eased by the sight of a letter in her mother's handwriting. Apprehensive of another application for money, she put it aside till she had met the housekeeper and reviewed several subjects with her: the weekly household accounts must be checked, Lady Bertram's diet modified, and arrangements made for a special treat at tea-time the following day – which would be the first time her aunt took a short walk outside since her illness. Stephen must be present to assist, and help contain Edmund's enthusiasm. Lady B, as Stephen called her, had already taken a little drive about the grounds in the trap with him and Edmund a few days ago. Fanny smiled to herself as she remembered the scene, and hoped all would go well the next day. She had to find solutions for three other household problems before escaping to the drawing-room.

Here her mother-in-law sat pondering over her correspondence, and did not disturb Fanny while she read her letter, except to ask for news of her sister. This request was not altogether an easy one, though Mrs Price's letter was not a long one, and did not give very much news, except to describe William's brief visit to the house in Portsmouth. Apart from maternal pride in how handsome he had become and what a kind son to his mother, there was nothing else that Fanny could read directly to Lady Bertram, as the entire second paragraph was taken up with a complaint about Betsey. It seemed that she had received a very advantageous offer of marriage from someone named Upton, the son of a wealthy tradesman in the town, which she had refused out of hand on the grounds that he was 'not romantic enough' in his address. Her mother feared that she was admitting the attentions of a certain young gentleman who was clearly *up to no good*, and Mrs Price demanded that Fanny write her sister at once to give her some serious advice, '*for nothing I can say to her will get her to attend to me. Rebecca reports that she has taken to meeting him secretly at the lending library and in the shops, and that he is trying to get her to accompany him to the Rooms one evening. I'm sure I don't know which way to turn, and wish that you could come home for a little while, just to knock some sense into her head.*'

Sighing as she folded away this missive, Fanny looked up to see her aunt watching her with a good deal of sympathy.

'Has my sister Price any new problem?'

Somewhat startled at her aunt's perceptiveness, Fanny briefly outlined the difficulty Mrs Price was having with her youngest child.

Lady Bertram nodded slowly before speaking:

'I sometimes wish all children could stay forever at the age of about nine – that is when they are so interesting and pleasant. I don't know what happens to them afterwards to turn them disagreeable and disobedient. It is a hard thing these days, being a parent.'

Fanny laughed gently. 'Do you really find Edmund so pleasant and interesting? I have heard you wish he were quieter and cleaner, on several occasions!'

Lady Bertram smiled. 'Edmund is a wonderful little boy, and so good to me … Only yesterday he told me he would never go to school, but stay with me here at Mansfield forever, till he was old enough to marry Alice Potts!'

'He knows very well that he was old enough to have gone in September, and that there will be little to prevent him from going next year. I am so pleased with the progress he has made recently with Stephen – do you think that Stephen will agree to continue following him till he goes to school?'

Lady Bertram smiled once more. 'Stephen may have other obligations long before that time comes – I cannot tell you how helpful that young man is, and how much I have come to appreciate his presence! I think Susan is an extremely lucky young woman, and I intend to see what I can do for them.' And taking off her spectacles, she took out her biscuit-tin for Pug's attention. It struck Fanny that Pug (of the third generation since she had come to the house) was also in the ninth year of his life, but that was insufficient to render him either interesting or pleasant.

12

*F*anny was surprised next morning by another letter in her mother's hand, but with the direction so ill-written that she was seized with misapprehension, and being alone in the room, lost no time in opening and reading it. It was brief and to the point:

Portsmouth, 25 Nov.

My dear Fanny,

I am afraid this letter brings nothing but bad news — Betsey has gone. She eloped last night with Philip Fitzjohn. They are bound for Scotland it seems — though no one here knows for sure. Rebecca says it has been preparing for days, and has had her ears soundly boxed for saying nothing directly of it to me. She has taken very little with her, and she has no money that I know of, so she will be entirely reliant upon his good graces.

I do not know what to do. I have written to William in London, although he told me last week that it will be impossible for him to leave headquarters for another fortnight at least. Fanny, use whatever resources you have to help your sister — if he does not marry her she is lost. If only Edmund were alive to force the marriage! Try to keep the whole affair as secret as possible — we must think of her good name.

Yr. loving mother,

Frances Price.

P.S. Do you think that Tom would help if you appealed to him?
She has taken the plant that you sent me, in the blue china pot. Richard Upton would have been a thousand times better.

Fanny read this missive through twice before arising hastily from the breakfast-table and running upstairs to her room, where she read it through very carefully for the third time before sitting down to think of what was best to do. Unsurprisingly, given the handwriting on the envelope, the letter had taken an extra day to arrive, though this was not an unusual occurrence with her mother's correspondence. In view of the circumstances, however, it reduced their eventual options, which she wanted to review before consulting Susan – London now seemed further away than ever before. She decided to write immediately to both William and Tom. She knew that the negotiations with which William's superior officer was involved had reached a crucial stage, but surely William could be released for a few days on family business? Tom must be appealed to for help in case the couple had decided on temporary residence in London as a cheap alternative to the long voyage northward, though she thought she knew enough of Tom and his wife to think they would exert the slightest effort on behalf of any member of her family. After she had written both these hasty letters she penned a third one, to her mother, enclosing some money for her immediate relief, and saying what she could in the way of encouragement:

I am certain she intends marriage, mother, my sister cannot be the sort of girl who would undertake such a journey for any other reason. Do you not think the plant presages domestic intentions of some sort? Anyway, we must contact as many potentially helpful people as possible, and pray that we have her news very soon.

She was aware of the lameness of this response even as she sealed it, but she gave the letters for posting and then went in search of her sister.

In the still-room both sisters wept an instant over Mrs Price's letter and comforted each other as best they could, though Susan was not as sanguine in her expectations as Fanny. She had greater experience of living conditions in the dismal little house in Portsmouth, of her mother's company and Rebecca's cooking, and could see very well why her sister was so anxious to escape from it at any cost.

'There is no chance for her, Fanny – what man would choose to marry a penniless girl, no matter how beautiful, if he could have her live with him for a few months?' Here her thoughts went immediately to Stephen, who she was certain would like to help in some way, but she could not imagine how. Susan did not know the identity of the Richard Upton her mother referred to, and Fanny herself needed an effort to recollect the young man she had mentioned in her last letter. This made Susan think of something else:

'But Fanny, if she wanted to leave the house at all costs, why not marry this Upton? He is a pleasing man and prosperous, according to our mother, and might have provided the solution to her problem of living at home.'

'Our sister may have read too many romances. She would very likely have married this young man and lived happily with him, had not the accident of her beauty and perhaps the flattery of young Fitzjohn given her the idea that she could do better for herself. Now she may easily find herself with nothing to hope for, at the age of seventeen!'

'It is so unfair – men may do as they please, and never have to face the consequences – '

'Certainly it is very unfair, Susan, but on the whole, life is not fair, and especially not to women. Which is why we must think hard of what we can do for our sister, now, while action may still be possible.'

A quarter of an hour's reflection, however, left them with only one immediate possibility: Susan could travel to Portsmouth and spend some weeks with their mother, to help her with the house and maintain her spirits until the outcome of Betsey's adventure was known. Several minutes' discussion convinced both sisters that this course of action was both right and necessary, and Fanny was very prepared to dig into her depleted reserves to ensure Susan a comfortable journey.

Whatever Susan's personal feelings at quitting Mansfield at this interesting time, perhaps for a month or more, and during the season of Christmas, she professed herself willing to leave the very next morning, asking only for the rest of the day to organise her departure and say her most urgent farewells. Fanny watched her sister leave to start her packing with a heavy heart, for she knew that life at Mansfield would not be easy without her. She did not need Edmund's watery inquiries about how aunt Susan would spend Christmas, nor Stephen Tilly's sombre expression at dinner, to remind her of the degree of sacrifice that Susan was making for a sister she barely knew. Before retiring that night she said goodbye to Susan – both had agreed it was unnecessary for her to awake for the dawn departure next morning. As much on Stephen's account as on any other, Fanny had acquiesced, so that Susan made her early start aided only by Stephen, with Jem along to give a hand with the box of provisions from Mansfield that Fanny had put aside for her mother.

Lady Bertram had not realised that Susan's departure would be as precipitate, and Fanny spent the whole morning with her, reasoning and soothing; yet the entire story was out and Fanny's patience depleted before she accepted the need for Susan's absence.

'But what good will Susan do at Portsmouth? She has not been there for over twelve years, and in any case a woman cannot be of much use in these matters. A gentleman must be found who will locate the couple and oblige them to marry – if only Tom were not so occupied at the moment! It is just the sort of thing his father was so good at.'

Fanny thought it kinder not to remind Lady Bertram of Sir Thomas' most notable failure in this line of activity. Her thoughts at this time were most often in Portsmouth with Susan and her mother, and her whole dependence each morning was on a letter from her sister. Yet three mornings went by in succession without news from any source, and on the fourth morning – when she did finally see a letter addressed to her – it proved to be from Mary in London.

It was probably too soon to expect a reply to her own letter asking for help, and she was not surprised to find that more than half of it was devoted to a description of her new relation's recent social triumph, and the hardships of the social round. It was not until the penultimate sentence that any mention was made of William:

We have not seen your brother lately but I know that he has recently been spending some time with Henry. This last hero, it appears, has gone visiting friends in the country. He will have more than enough of the country at Mansfield, I wager, if I can persuade him to accompany us on our Christmas visit, when we look forward to seeing you all again.

Although she read this paragraph twice, Fanny did not have the time for more than a throb of apprehension at the prospect of the coming Christmas at Mansfield. Mary had made no mention of her mother-in-law's health, and in addition it seemed that either Tom had not received her letter about Betsey, or had chosen not to mention its contents to his wife. William had not yet answered her own desperate appeal, though she took comfort in the certainty that he was doing whatever lay in his power to help his sister. Her main hope now lay in news from Susan, who must write soon.

As is the case with anyone who anxiously waits for news, Fanny gave little proof of patience, though she showed some ingenuousness in the reasons she invented for the letters that did not arrive. When she tired of evoking the tardiness of the posts, there was always the weather, bad roads and unscrupulous messengers. By the sixth day after Susan's departure her mind was moving along more sinister lines, foreboding a tragic eventuality or even a cataclysm involving one or more members of her family. In the circumstances, work seemed the only palliative – and late that morning she remembered that she had accepted to decorate the church for the coming Sunday, and set out in the trap suitably encumbered with bunches of holly, dried flowers and apples. She spent a peaceful and productive hour making two enormous bouquets, and having sent Jem on a shopping expedition to the village, set out on the walk back to Mansfield and luncheon.

As she passed the Parsonage, however, the front door opened and the incumbent of Mansfield appeared, with hospitality writ large across his countenance, and with expansive gestures to match. Accosting her at the gate, he invited her into the house 'for a modest collation – a mere nothing, but given as those give who give from the heart' – here he broke off, his face fiery with whatever emotion was increasing his native incoherence.

Fanny was embarrassed. She thought it a gesture of simple kindness to accept some small part of this bounty, and had she been accompanied by Susan, or even by Edmund, she would have been inclined to enter the house for a little while. In the present circumstances, however, she decided against it, and together with many nods and gestures, she gave the good doctor to understand that she must lose no time in getting home, where she was urgently awaited. Somewhat to her surprise, Dr Thwaite darted back to the house, seized his cloak from the inside of the door, and returned to accompany her on the walk back to Mansfield, offering her his arm as they set forward.

However vexatious she felt this tête-à-tête to be, there was nothing for it but to suffer it with a good grace, walking as rapidly as she could, and talking incessantly on impersonal subjects. She had reviewed the condition of vestments, hymn-books and kneelers, and was ready to embark on the subject of Christmas dinner for the needy, when they reached the side entrance of the house, and Edmund emerged, running forward with his hoop and calling out his welcome.

It was impossible at this point not to extend a luncheon invitation to her companion, though Fanny felt sharply irritated at the complacent smile with which it was accepted. Fortunately, Lady Bertram was in fine spirits during the meal, and conversed at length on her favourite subject – the missions – desiring to consult Dr Thwaite after luncheon on how some of her recent needlework could be most usefully deployed. Fanny gratefully escaped to her boudoir, for by this time she had a headache that needed a half-hour's rest in the darkened room.

How much time had she wasted that morning – and how little had she achieved, germane to her present purpose of helping Betsey! Every endeavour seemed hopeless, and she lay in the dark feeling very miserable, with tears of unhappiness oozing slowly from her eyes. How hard it was to be a woman! If she could have been a man only for a few days, could she not clear this situation – at least, do something more than lie here helplessly? She took comfort in the thought that William was surely doing something, and would write to her soon, and on this thought she slept.

She awoke to a darkened sky, having slept for several hours. The maid was tapping at her door, wanting to light the fire, and on her going downstairs to the drawing-room, she saw two letters for herself on the hall table. They were in Susan's handwriting.

13

*T*he first letter ran thus:

Little Street, 7 Dec.

My dear Fanny,
  They had no news at all from London when I reached here yesterday evening, having had a comfortable journey, but still tired, and very thankful for a bed after the jolting of the stage. Mother and Rebecca both mighty glad to see me, and full of attentions, but no better organised than in the past.
  This morning we had a letter from William. He has done a great deal, as you can imagine, and I was able at last to offer real comfort to our mother, following which I came here to our old bedroom to write this to you.
  This is his news: finding it impossible to obtain permission for even a few days' home-leave, he cast about him in London, and searched amongst his friends for anyone likely to know Philip Fitzjohn's family, and his possible whereabouts. After only a day's search, he was very fortunate to fall in with an old acquaintance who had been at Oxford with Fitzjohn's older brother, who knew of some lodgings rented by the family in Jermyn Street. This friend actually accompanied William there on two occasions (the couple being from home, on their first visit), and William was able to talk at length to Betsey, on this and on a subsequent visit, though to no great effect. It seems they had no intentions of an early marriage, I am sorry to say, and Betsey had far more feeling to express on the subject of Astley's Amphitheatre than on any point of misconduct either on her own or on her lover's account.
  What can I say, Fanny? Her only excuse is youth and thought-

lessness, but such a total absence of rectitude must be attributed, I fear, to some serious lapse in education. I spoke to our mother last evening for almost two hours, she is very cut up by Betsey's behaviour. As you know, our sister was always her favourite child, and she cannot understand why all this has happened.

William reported that Betsey had no notion of returning home in the near future, but a stern letter from Fitzjohn senior, received in Jermyn Street a few hours before William's third visit to Betsey, changed the entire situation. The young man was instantly recalled home, under threat of the customary sanctions, and ordered to leave Betsey to her own devices. He was apparently very shocked, having given out at home that he was at the races, and imagining his family in the dark. Seeing him prepared, however reluctantly, to obey the parental injunction, the scales fell from Betsey's eyes, and William described a tempestuous scene, which ended with her determination to return home immediately. We expect her hourly, though I am apprehensive at her travelling alone – it is a long journey, and William cannot accompany her.

Richard Upton visited the house yesterday evening, though I cannot say that he had very much to say to me. Rebecca says that he is here on most evenings, looking for news of Betsey. It seems he scarcely says a word to anyone, 'but just sits in the parlour like a beaten dog, drinking cup after cup of tea'. Which if you can remember the contents of Rebecca's tea-tray, is considerable proof of devotion. He seems such a nice young man, Fanny (and not at all ill-looking, though not handsome), that I allow myself to hope that he may be persuaded to take her in the end, though mother says that Betsey was very proud and ill-mannered in her rejection of him.

As you can imagine, I miss you all and Mansfield more than I can express – the house here is so ill-ordered and uncomfortable that I wonder how I lived here for so many years without running mad. Everything seems smaller and more neglected than before. Fanny, I know I could live content in a two-roomed cottage, given the right company [these words were heavily emphasised], but I would need to order things precisely if I wanted to be happy. Here there is nothing but confusion.

The box of stores you sent is proving invaluable, we had some shav-

84

ings of the sweet ham for luncheon, and Mr Upton had mince pies with his tea last evening. I shall write you again tomorrow.

Yr. loving sister,

Susan.

With fingers grown clumsy from impatience, Fanny tore open the second letter, and read the following:

8 Dec.

Dearest Fanny,

    Our sister has come – she reached here two hours ago, travelling in the coach of William's friend, who left her at the door with her portmanteau and a servant-girl, but it seems he will return tomorrow for our thanks and Rebecca's tea. Thank God there are some true Christians in the world!

    I was somewhat taken aback by the appearance of Betsey. She is indeed a beautiful girl, looking far older than her age, and resembling nothing so much as the miniature of Maria Bertram in the morning-room at Mansfield. She had very little to say for herself, being very tired and tearful, and is still shut up in her room. Let us pray that the experiences of the past weeks will be a life-long lesson to her, for it seems likely that her romantic notions have taken a sad bruising. More tomorrow evening, which is the preferred time for writing, offering the best chance of quiet, though I must remember to obtain some candles tomorrow – I had forgotten how difficult it is to do any sort of work with the light of these tallow ones.

9 Dec.

I am once more writing in our little bedroom upstairs, which has so many memories of your only visit to this town! Our mother has gone out to church – where she goes most evenings of late – and Rebecca is out walking with her intended. Betsey is downstairs in the parlour talking to Mr Upton and William's friend, who arrived more than an hour ago, and has agreed to stay for supper. I was somewhat embarrassed at offering him the hospitality of the house until we met, and I remembered that he has been a guest at this house in the past.

85

He is none other than the Mr Crawford – Mary's brother – who came visiting once, many years ago, as you can surely recollect. You met him recently at Everingham, I remember, so you will not be overly surprised at his presence here. He brought our parent a letter from William, according to which he has been all kindness, and it is thanks to his good offices that our sister is now snug at home, and not on the streets in London. It seems he did everything. Knowing Fitzjohn's brother, he located the couple for William, visited with him, conducted Betsey here, and Fanny (here I literally weep for joy) – he has already offered to take me to London with him when he returns in a few days, which will give me the chance of returning to Mansfield with the others, in time for Christmas.

I know you will be glad (and I hope you will not be the only one) at the idea of my return home for the Season – I miss you all greatly.

Now for Betsey – she eats and sleeps but little, and is still somewhat disfigured with sleeplessness and much weeping, but today she is calmer. Our mother says she has lost her looks, which I find hard to credit, but if that is indeed the case these can be restored with time. It is now up to her family and friends to attempt to compensate her for what cannot be restored, and, God willing, to ensure that she builds a basis for more rational behaviour in future.

She has not spoken very much to me, but that is understandable, for she scarcely remembers me. She talks freely enough with Richard Upton, however, and with Major Crawford, although she holds him in some awe. I can hear their voices as I sit here writing, it seems an animated conversation. I must stop writing and go downstairs to the kitchen, where Rose (who accompanied Betsey from London, and whom I have hired for the moment, until she returns with me) is looking to the roasting of some chickens, and warming up a large meat-pie from Mansfield. It will not be what either of the gentlemen is accustomed to, but better than what normally prevails here.

I will write again as soon as I have a moment,

Yrs. affectionately,

Susan.

Fanny read this letter feverishly, her feelings indescribably confused her mind almost refusing to credit the written words that she read

86

At first amazement was uppermost – why had Henry Crawford done this? She recollected his extraordinary efforts to get William his lieutenancy, and the way he had visited her in Portsmouth merely to ensure that she was comfortable. Here her mind insisted that there was an excellent reason at the time – he had professed himself ardently in love with her.

But now? She looked about the quiet library to which she had escaped to read her letters in peace, and stared along the dim rows of titles as though they could provide an answer. Now, there was nothing between herself and Henry Crawford. Her prematurely ended marriage, his ancient error and his years of adventure had ensured that they met again as strangers, with nothing significant to say to each other. Yet why would a man like Henry Crawford go to such lengths to help William (whom he scarcely knew) to rescue his younger sister – a total stranger? She had insufficient vanity and far too much sense to think that he still cherished any sentiment for her, beyond possibly a vague regret. There was perhaps another reason – could it be that he regretted his behaviour towards the Bertrams and wished to make a gesture of atonement? A very few seconds' consideration showed this reasoning for the nonsense it was: quite apart from the fact that he was as much entitled to consider that the Bertrams rather owed *him* some gesture of atonement, Betsey was in no sense a Bertram (except perhaps in appearance), and he owed the Prices nothing, in fact, quite the contrary. His good action towards William had been helping in the promotion of the two younger Prices, and William's family could never be brought to see him other than as a benefactor of the first order.

She now understood that William and his 'friend' had indeed spent the week in London searching for their sister, and saw in a new light some of the delicacy of their negotiations. In the first outpouring of gratitude she determined to write to her brother immediately, and to her mother and Susan by the same post. Here a voice whispered to her that if she were to give thanks where they were rightly due she owed Henry a letter before anyone else, but she trembled with embarrassment at the very notion of addressing herself to him on paper, thanking him for what he had almost certainly never intended as a personal favour to herself. She sat debating this point with herself for nearly half an hour, her mind growing increasingly confused instead of clearer, her concluding thought being that she needed a thorough, calm review of the situation before doing anything; but that it was probably necessary for at least one member of the Price family to formally express gratitude for the service rendered to Betsey. This letter need not be very lengthy, or even a personal one, she would need to phrase it very carefully.

On this thought she arose and went in search of Stephen, who should rightly be the first to learn of Susan's impending return. Lady Bertram could hear the good news at dinner, and Edmund, in view of the excitement and noise that it would generate, had best wait to hear the news till next morning.

14

During the whole of that night and the following day, Fanny's mind was in the little house at Portsmouth. With the passage of the hours, she felt an even stronger impulse of gratitude for disaster averted – she realised that whether or not the obliging Mr Upton finally married her youngest sister, her family owed Betsey's restoration to them to an act of disinterested kindness that far outweighed Henry Crawford's first favour to the Prices. She now regretted having written on the subject to Tom. Having avoided the worst, she would have preferred to try and keep the whole matter a secret, as much for the sake of Betsey as for anyone else – she hoped that Susan's future happiness could not be adversely affected by a younger sister's foolish mistake. A short message from Tom the next morning later shed fresh light on this:

Sincerely sorry about Betsey – as you can imagine, we are somewhat pinched for both time and money at present (bills still coming in daily after the reception!) and I had much rather not disturb Mary with any bad news in her present delicate state. Though it was impossible to keep the news from my brother-in-law, who was with me when your letter arrived. I imagine he spoke to William of it, and you can surely count on your own brother to do whatever he can for you.

He at last mentioned his mother, professing himself sincerely happy at her rapid recovery, and sincerely looking forward to seeing the whole family united at Mansfield for Christmas. Fanny wondered whether the word 'sincere' carried an entirely different connotation in some vocabularies, or whether it was merely that Tom had adopted some of his wife's attitudes. She recalled that he had always been selfish, but since his marriage seemed to have added obtuseness to egotism.

Although she had written immediately to William and Susan, and although her strong feeling of obligation to thank Henry persisted, the crucial letter had not yet been written. Fanny had written and re-written it mentally a score of times, and even when she started writing it, she drafted three different versions, rejected on the grounds of sounding either too effusive or too cold. The fourth version read:

Mansfield, 13 Dec.

Dear Major Crawford,

   Much as it embarrasses me to have to write to you on family business, I cannot omit this chance of expressing not only my personal gratitude, but that of every member of my family for your unparalleled kindness to our youngest sister, and I know that were it known among the Bertrams, they would wish to add their thanks to those of the Prices.

   I look forward to meeting you at Christmas, when I can thank you in person.

Yrs. etc.

Fanny Bertram.

Fanny was not satisfied with this masterpiece of the epistolary art. She had spent almost an hour on the last sentence – at first it appeared as a bold invitation to Mansfield, on a second reading it seemed vapid and over-formal, on a third unnecessarily personal, and so on. She crossed out and rephrased repeatedly before returning to the original version – but it was not yet posted. She might need another day's reflection for that, but on reflection she thought it had much better go as it was, considering the amount of time it had taken to write.

Sitting at her writing-desk, she searched in every drawer for a stick of sealing-wax, for it looked as though Edmund had been busy among her papers again – as witnessed by a wonderful carriage and four drawn in bright colours, in which were seated a smiling 'Edmund', 'Mama', and 'Susan', with 'Stephen' perched up in front as coachman – the ultimate accolade! Unnecessarily signed 'Edmund Bertram Esq.' in large capitals, this composition carried as bonus a portrait of Timmy in the margin, with flourishing whiskers and curling tail that surpassed that of the horses. Fanny spent several minutes examining her son's universe, and smiled to herself as she continued her search. Not finding what she sought, she continued opening the little drawers concealed in the upper portion of the desk, where she sometimes kept nibs, coloured ink, tacks, string, court-plaister and a pen-knife, which was also missing – and which she rather thought was in the company of the missing stick of sealing-wax.

She continued her absent-minded search, opening and shutting increasingly smaller spaces – some mere cubby-holes – till at last she admitted defeat and turned away from the desk, but in doing so her eye fell upon a sliver of paper sticking out from beneath that upper section of the desk that rested upon the surface of the table. Evidently dislodged by her rummaging, it seemed very old and dirty, and without much curiosity she drew it out with the intention of throwing it away. Glancing at it before crumpling it, she was startled to find it closely written in a vaguely familiar hand. It was only after reading several lines that she realised that she held a page torn from a diary, and that the handwriting was that of her cousin Maria.

'and the warm pressure of our hands closely linked. Who cares whether the words are generally nonsense and sometimes vulgar, so we can stand thus, and look into one another's eyes?

He has completed the sketches for my head, and cannot decide whether to execute it in oils as a miniature, which would take at least three weeks, or as a larger line drawing, a matter of about two days. I prefer the prospect of the miniature, as being somehow more significant, and tried to get his promise on this, but he refused to be pinned down, it seems he did not think himself ready as yet for anything of such consequence, and cannot commit himself as to time.

(Remember to borrow some of mama's French perfume for the dress-rehearsal this evening.)

Later – the totally unexpected has happened – my father has returned

91

*– simply walked into our rehearsal, back from the ends of the earth!
'Old Tom', as Julia calls him, might as well have been 'Old Nick' for
the éclat of his entry, and the speed with which the playhouse closed and
players dispersed. But tonight I am all excitement and expectation, for
surely he must come tomorrow to see my father. I dream already of
dismissing Count Cassel to his estates forever, and spending the rest of
my life looking into Henry's dark eyes. Sometimes I have a feeling of
unease when I think of his reputation, and his behaviour to Julia, or
when I see silly Fanny looking at us with her air of virtuous reproach;
but he has only to smile at me for every rational thought to fly out of
my head.*

    O God! how to wait till tomorrow?

*15 Oct. He never came! There must be some terrible mistake – I spent
the entire afternoon devising schemes for going over to the Parsonage to
find out what was wrong – maybe he is ill. Surely they will visit this
evening, and then we can – '*

Only one side of the paper was legible, on the other it was faded
and turned so grey with damp and mildew that it was not possible
even to decipher whether it was the previous or the following page
from the one she had just read, with shaking fingers. She became
aware of her own rapid breathing as she read the page once more,
and felt the years roll back, to the evening when Sir Thomas had
walked into their dress-rehearsal, just arrived from Antigua and
impatient to see his family.

She could remember their consternation – the thrill of fear with
which she heard Julia's announcement that he was already in the
hall, and the speed with which the Crawfords withdrew to the
Parsonage, taking Baron Wildenhaim with them for the evening.
She could not recall with as much clarity what had happened on
the next day, having been far too preoccupied with her own position in relation to the theatricals, and wondering how her uncle
would receive her; but she remembered a courtesy visit from Henry
Crawford soon after, calling with Dr Grant to say goodbye on his
way somewhere, and could remember her concern at how Maria
would react to this piece of news. Maria's reaction had been
one of pride and resentment; she had expedited her marriage to

Mr Rushworth in order to show Henry Crawford that her happiness did not depend on him.

That afternoon Fanny took another solitary walk to her seat in the silent woods. The day was cold, with an icy wind and the hint of impending snow in the implacable grey sky. Sadly she took out the page from Maria's diary, tearing it into shreds before raking it underfoot together with the withered leaves that lay everywhere. It had slept wedged beneath the shelf of that desk for so many years, since the days when the room had belonged to the eldest daughter of the house, whose imperious beauty, wealth and splendid alliance had made her the cynosure of Mansfield society. Fanny expended several moments on such gentle philosophical musings before being driven homewards by the wind.

Although just after four o'clock, darkness was coming down, and in the distant house she saw candles already being lit in some rooms. For the first time she asked herself – was there more to existence than simply this: returning to a warm comfortable house, where one's family awaited with an afternoon meal?

Fanny was at this time conscious of an immense latent curiosity about places and people. She had lived more or less continuously at Mansfield – with recent yearly interludes at the dull dark house in Huntingdon – since she was ten years old, and by now had a growing urge to move outside. When the world contained so many places to visit, people to meet, and so much to see, for how much longer could she live within the same charmed circle? She did not seek within herself the cause for such a radical change in attitude. Instead she decided as a first step that if William was stationed in England, she would pay him a visit in London early in the new year, and maybe even go down with him to Portsmouth. It would be pleasant to see her mother again, and Betsey. Wondering about her future, at Mansfield or elsewhere, she was led to think on Edmund's choice of a future school. The subject of Edmund reminded her of her rifled desk, and as serious thought is known to stimulate appetite, she looked forward to an excellent meal, as well as an opportunity of settling accounts with that young man.

***

After dinner that night Stephen approached her hesitantly, saying he had a small problem that he wished to discuss with her. He felt that in view of the imminent arrival of Julia and her family, as well as the lord of the Park and his entourage, it might be convenient for him to return to the Parsonage for the present. Fanny was slightly taken aback, and immediately gave him to understand that she viewed his suggestion somewhat dimly. There was no dearth of bedrooms at Mansfield, the housekeeper and staff had Christmas preparations well under control, and could handle a larger number of guests than were expected. He was still quite invaluable in helping with Lady Bertram's regime, as well as keeping Edmund profitably occupied for the greater part of the day. Finally, if Susan were to return to Mansfield to find him exiled to the Parsonage, she did not want to be responsible for the consequences. It was enough. Blushing and stammering with pleasure, Stephen gave her to understand that he was at her service for as long as she needed him.

She recalled the last part of this conversation when reading a letter from Susan the next day, for her sister's first inquiry was about Stephen, and she rejoiced in the prospect of their first Christmas together at Mansfield. She also gave Fanny news of their mother:

> She seems a changed woman, grown very silent, though I know deeply grateful for Betsey's return. She hardly leaves the house now except to go to church, and has taken up patchwork-quilting in her spare time, of which she has some at last, for I look after the housekeeping, as you can imagine. She is very happy about Stephen, and asked me to say so to you, with apologies for not having written sooner. It is now that I realise how similar she is to our aunt Bertram, and not only in appearance, but also in a few mannerisms, nervous reactions and occasionally in her way of thinking – it is a pity that they have grown so apart over the years.

Susan had more to say about the assiduous Mr Upton, but no precise information as yet on the date of her return home, though she had something to add about Henry Crawford:

> May I say how much I appreciate him? He has such a sympathetic personality and such agreeable manners, yet I think from his bearing he must have the habit of command. When I think of his behaviour to our family, I am filled with such gratitude towards him as I have

94

only felt for very few people in my life, and you can guess who some of those are,

Yr. grateful sister,

Susan.

Mrs Price had added a message for her daughter:

All is very well here with us at the moment, dear Fanny, and as you can imagine, Susan is a great comfort and help to me. She will make Mr Tilly an excellent wife, I pray that he is deserving of her. Betsey continues well, though I do not think she is happy, for all the hours spent in discussion with R. Upton, who has taken to argumentation, whereas before he was more amenable. Where will all this end? I doubt at the altar, though I leave everything in the hands of God, and pray daily for my family, and such good friends as Mjr Crawford has shown himself to be — the more pity that you could not bring yourself to marry him. Send me news of little Edmund, and my sister Bertram, who I hope does better, and whom I would dearly like to see again.

After reading this, Fanny looked up with a smile, to encounter the look of her aunt, who had just finished reading one of her own letters.

'This is from Tom – it seems his wife's health is so precarious as to endanger their visit next week, but he announces the arrival of Julia and family for the day after tomorrow.'

'Does he mention Susan?'

'No … is she still in Portsmouth? How is she to return home?'

Fanny blushed slightly: 'Major Crawford was to have taken her to London – '

In the resounding silence that followed, Fanny realised that there was nothing for it now but to tell Lady Bertram everything, not only of what Henry Crawford had just done for her niece, but, of far greater consequence – what had been the true history of his relations with her eldest daughter. It was a conversation that took up the rest of the morning.

15

It was difficult to set eyes on Julia Yates without experiencing nostalgia for the era of the fig-leaf. She was one of those women for whom the pursuit of elegance occupies every waking moment, sometimes to the detriment of rationality, and often with very indifferent results. One might expect such a reckless expense of energy and ingenuity to produce a greater effect, but she was still a sickly looking creature, expensively dressed, and with very little to say for herself.

Always inferior to Maria in beauty and accomplishments, Julia had taken refuge in fashion at a tender age, and one of Fanny's earliest memories of her was her prodigious collection of bows and sashes. Grown to womanhood, she had watched her older sister charm the first man she had loved, and had consoled herself with her superior sense of style. After her hasty wedding to the Hon. John Yates, precipitated by Maria's elopement with Henry, she continued to find her main satisfaction in a reputation for good taste, attempting to compensate for the inward deficiency of personality by a preoccupation with external appearance. Her fragile exterior concealed a tough constitution, for no journeyman or hired labourer worked a harder or a longer day than she did, rising very often at dawn, and burning the midnight oil in the pursuit of the latest sleeve, or the cleverest hairstyle.

Fanny, who had not seen her since Edmund's funeral, was unprepared for so much elegance, having missed the essential transformation from healthy young woman to social butterfly, and blinked at the vision descending from the coach, followed by her two daughters dressed in matching toilettes. Yates himself only emerged several minutes later, being delayed by the off-loading of an unconscionable number of boxes and bags, for the feminine branch of the Yates family travelled with a minimal wardrobe that necessitated the use of a supplementary vehicle.

Julia showed every sign of pleasure at meeting Fanny again:

'Ah, Fanny – nice to see you again. And good to be back at Mansfield! Jane, Maria, come and meet your cousin Fanny, Uncle Edmund's wife. Jane, show Fanny your curtsey.'

Jane and Maria were dressed as perfect replicas of their mother, from fur-lined bonnets and pelisses to uncomfortable-looking boots, and both had imitated their mother in adopting a conscious air of fashion, comical in the young, for Maria was only seven years old, and Jane four years older.

Jane looked very like the young Julia Fanny remembered from her childhood at Mansfield – tall, ethereally blonde and blue-eyed, to all outward appearances a very pattern-card of perfection. Maria showed more promise, being puny, carrot-haired, and having a naughty twinkle in her eye. This was confirmed the very next morning, when she saw Maria run shrieking down the main staircase chased by Edmund and Pug, and later from the drawing-room window watched them running about the whitened lawns, their mufflers flying behind them.

Fanny was regretting not having thought to settle them in the Old Wing, where there were several empty rooms, for Julia it seemed needed more than one to house her wardrobe. She had brought her maid, but had to share her mother's hairdresser, though she did Jane's hair herself, and from appearances it seemed Jane did Maria's hair, which stuck out in pigtails from under whatever fashionable headgear her mother had decreed.

Despite the disparity in age and sex, Maria and Edmund were comrades within a day of meeting, both slavish admirers of Timmy, who by now was big enough to run about the house unsupervised, testing his claws with impunity upon upholstery and curtains. A state of warfare was rapidly developing between him and Pug, who tolerated no invasion of the drawing-room, and matters had reached a point where Fanny had ordered Edmund not to bring his pet downstairs unless Pug was out of doors. This Edmund viewed as unjust, and he had taken to carrying the kitten about in his pocket, to which compromise Fanny had tacitly agreed. In consequence the two cousins were soon to be seen in frequent confabulation over the welfare of Timmy, or engaged in some game that necessitated his participation.

Jane obviously viewed this friendship, not to mention the covert presence of the young cat in the drawing-room, with disapprobation. Looking around and seeing that Fanny had left the room, she remarked to her mother:

'Mama, cousin Edmund does not have very good manners, does he?'

'No, dearest, but then we must understand that he has no father.'

Jane turned to her grandmother, seated on her sofa, and busy with her fringing.

'Grandmother, is that why he is allowed to carry that cat about?'

'I don't think so. Maybe it's because he hasn't many friends at Mansfield, and as you know, children need friends.'

'*I don't.*'

There was nothing to say to this, and Lady Bertram returned to her fringing, but her daughter Julia had not yet done.

'Mama, why has Edmund not gone to school as yet? He must be nearly ten by now.'

'He is just nine, though tall for his age. He will go to school next year.'

'Fanny must do something about his manners – obviously he is encouraged to do as he pleases in the house here. And as for his clothes!'

'I have always found him a polite child, though not always very quiet, but that is something else. When Susan is at home, she keeps him under tighter control than his mother, and recently he has spent a lot of time outdoors with Mr Tilly. I daresay Fanny will get him some new clothes for school next year.'

'Fanny should get *herself* some clothes. I would be ashamed to appear in the thing she was wearing this morning. It looked to be at least three years old!'

'It was probably older, for Fanny does not often buy herself new things, but I think she is so pretty, and is always so charming that I never notice what she wears.'

Julia said no more – she could not be expected to concur with the divine proposition that the body is more than the raiment, nor could she fathom the thought processes of someone who did not notice what people wore. She detected a subtle change in her mother, who seemed to have aged disconcertingly. Though still inclined to loll on her sofa for the greater part of the day, she now sometimes took a slow walk outdoors on a fine afternoon, and whereas in the past she had never voiced her opinions, or indeed had any opinions to voice, especially in the presence of her family; at dinner last night she had twice heard her mother speak her mind on a subject, once in flat contradiction of her son-in-law.

Fanny was just as unexpected. Though still very quiet and retiring in manner, her pleasant smile seemed to come more often than Julia remembered, lighting up her face and revealing her as an unusually attractive young woman, in despite of her clothes. Julia wondered whether there was any truth in the story she had heard about Dr Thwaite, and decided to be on the lookout. Her husband could see no sense in such a rumour:

'The old boy must be well over fifty! And your cousin Fanny is a young woman, and not bad-looking, either.'

'She would look a whole lot better if she looked more to herself. I hear Dr Thwaite is a personable man, of independent means, well-connected, and would be an excellent stepfather to Edmund, who is in sad need of some discipline. What could be more suitable for Fanny, situated as she is?'

John Yates did not find this conversation interesting enough to pursue, but at last ventured:

'Someone younger, certainly. What say you to Major Crawford? We heard from that niece of Simpson's in Bath that the fellow is a nabob now, and still unmarried.'

But for some reason his wife would not hear of such a thing.

'For goodness' sake, never mention the possibility to anyone in this house! The consequences would be incalculable!'

'Oh pooh, my dear – I have no patience with your consequences! And you know very well, from what Tom wrote us after his marriage, about the infamous elopement – '

'I don't want to *talk* about this any more. Now, what are your plans for tomorrow?'

John Yates' main pastime was hunting, which he had little enough opportunity of practising in Bath, and which had constituted the main attraction of Mansfield at this time of the year. He was waiting patiently for the arrival of his host, or of any other gentleman who would accompany him outdoors, having ascertained that neither Dr Thwaite nor his nephew were of any use in this respect. Until then he was at the disposal of his wife, who had planned a round of visits to the neighbouring houses, and he had to endure four more afternoons of these before the arrival of Sir Thomas Bertram and his wife.

It was exactly seven days before Christmas when they drove up at last, on the afternoon of a clear blue day, the more temperate for the light snowfall of the previous night. The carriage stopped before the entrance; Mary Bertram descended leisurely, and stood looking up at the house as she waited for her husband to give her his arm up the steps. Baddeley stood in attendance in the doorway with Manners, their speeches of welcome prepared. Fanny knew that she should go down to welcome the master and mistress of the house, and she intended to do so. But something prevented her, so that she clung to the banister of the landing with a beating heart and leaden feet, looking down into the hallway as Tom and his wife entered the house, searching beyond them for Susan. She saw the door of the drawing-room open, and Julia move forward to greet her brother, with Yates close behind, and she saw Mary's maid enter the open doorway carrying a large box, followed by another woman who looked to be a dresser or perhaps a nurse – but where was Susan? The carriage pulled away to the side of the house, the front door closed, and Fanny bent her head over the carved wood, swallowing her disappointment before forcing herself to go downstairs to join in the greetings.

★★★

The drawing-room was brightly lit. Everyone seemed to be talking together, there was laughter and kind inquiries on every side, but she found it hard to distinguish individual words – the room was a mass of dim and confused sound in the midst of which she moved – until she heard Lady Bertram ask a question:

'*But where is Susan?*'

Fanny had the impression that the question was followed by an echoing stillness, which lasted for several seconds before Mary answered:

'Susan? Well, there was the problem of finding her a place in our carriage, with all the luggage and four persons to accommodate, so Henry offered to bring her with him when he arrives in a couple of days, and to bring my harp as well.'

Here Tom took over from his wife:

'I hope nothing occurs to keep them in London – some of the roads are quite bad already. They know they must be here before Monday, for when we are planning something, which I shall tell you all about tomorrow.'

The room righted itself, conversation became coherent. Fanny was surprised at how relieved she felt at the prospect of Susan arriving in time for Christmas, and she smiled her relief at Stephen, who looked as though he had just had a somewhat similar experience.

Julia, in the meanwhile, had been eyeing Mary with a mixture of distaste and envy. Mary looked rosier and more blooming than ever – there was no doubt of her condition by this time, and it suited her. But Julia's eye had been taken by the splendid furs that her new sister wore, that merited a compliment.

'These? They are ermine, bought for me in Moscow by a friend at the Embassy there. They were fairly expensive, I believe, nothing like the prices we paid for Russian furs just after the War.'

Fanny heard this with an inward smile, illustrating as it did the relationship between the two women. Accustomed as she was to being an arbiter of fashion in an English watering-town, Julia was no match for someone like Mary. Although Mary's wardrobe could not compare in size to that of her new sister-in-law, every piece of it was authentic, expensive, or carried its own anecdote. If her furs were Russian, her boots were Italian and Spanish, her jewels came from select houses all over Europe, and her dresses were usually bought in Paris. Julia was obliged to console herself with the thought that she at least did not resemble a pudding, and that for the duration of her entire stay at Mansfield, she need never wear the same outfit twice.

Fanny was not seated beside Mary that evening, and consequently never had the opportunity to exchange even a few words on the subject of Susan's stay in London, although Mary smiled at her once across the table – a smile of complicity and promise. And so Fanny sat up late that night with a book, and Mary's knock at her door was not entirely unexpected.

'Were you waiting up for me? I have such a *lot* to tell you, but not today. I am dead from tiredness after the drive, and Sir Edward has prescribed a minimum of ten hours' rest, so I will not keep you up. But here are some messages for you – ' and she put three envelopes down on Fanny's bedside table. A few more moments of idle talk, of Susan's helpfulness and William's charm (or was it the other way around?) and especially of her own condition and how keen she was to see an end to it, and she was gone – the door closing behind her and the sound of her laugh as Fanny seized on her letters.

Both Susan's and William's were mere notes, sending her every good wish in case their reunion was delayed till after the Season. Both breathed relief at the happy conclusion of affairs in Portsmouth, and both breathed fervent thanks to the family benefactor. The third letter was from the benefactor himself, and was even briefer than the others:

> *Russell Street, 17 Dec.*
>
> My dear Mrs Bertram,
>   *I was pleased to receive your kind message, which though entirely unnecessary, yet gives me the opportunity of saying that I, too, look forward to Christmas at Mansfield this year.*
>
> Yrs. etc.,
>
> Henry Crawford.

16

*A*s promised, Tom made his announcement at breakfast the next morning: two days before Christmas, Mansfield would host a 'musical soirée', consisting of a concert followed by supper and a ball for every family of consequence in the neighbourhood. This would serve the purpose of inaugurating the Christmas season, and the listeners guessed that it would incidentally restore the lord and lady of Mansfield to their rightful position as leaders of the small rural society, a position somewhat compromised by his frequent absences in the past. It was the first Christmas in many years that Tom had spent at the Park, and he planned to do it in style. About two and twenty families would be invited, cards of invitation were already prepared and ready for distribution. Since in general country people were not in the habit of such gatherings at this time of the year, between snobbishness, boredom and curiosity the Bertrams could be pretty sure of a positive response.

Fanny listened in some surprise – this move did not logically follow the tone of Tom's recent letters and his concern for Mary's health. Eventually she ventured a gentle comment to the effect that the effort of organising and hosting such a function might prove exhausting to the new mistress of Mansfield, whom they understood to be in a delicate condition.

Tom overrode this instantly: naturally, his wife's health was a paramount concern, to him of all people. The family was given to understand that, far from organising anything, Mary Bertram would be required to be nothing more than a simple spectator – the only effort that would be asked of her on that evening would be to open the dancing at the ball. Tom undertook to organise the entire evening himself, with the aid of one or two members of the family (here there was a glance at Fanny and Julia), and since the essential work of organisation had already been done by himself, he did not see where the problem lay.

Fanny sighed. Once more, masculine logic and elementary lack of imagination would throw the greater part of the work on to a few unfortunate women. Still, if there really was to be a ball within five days, no time was to be lost. To be fair, Tom had done *some* preparation, for in addition to writing the invitation-list he had contacted the family caterers, and a group of musicians and a singer from Nottingham were already engaged for the evening. Clearly, this would constitute the sum of his collaboration.

In the course of a morning interview Mrs Manners made it clear that her own preparations for Christmas were comprehensive enough, and could not include the entire responsibility for such a function, though naturally she was prepared to offer every assistance in her power. Fanny was eventually able to enlist her co-operation in helping to hire additional staff for the evening, and in the opening and cleaning of the ball-room and reception rooms. Fanny realised that the rest of the work necessary for preparing the evening was to fall upon herself, whose experience was severely limited, having only once before attended a formal ball in the entire course of her life.

Julia early announced that she had a great deal of personal preparation to make for the evening, not really having come prepared with a sufficiently *grande toilette* adequate for such an occasion. (*How like Tom to be so inconsiderate!*) Still, in five days something respectable might be achieved, which did not leave her much time for anything else, though eventually she was persuaded to agree to look after the floral decorations for the ball-room, and the supper and card-rooms. Susan's absence was sorely felt by her sister, in a major part for the help and moral support she would have provided at this time. Stephen was very willing to help in any capacity, but he was more necessary than ever in keeping Edmund and his cousins occupied for a good deal of the day, though lessons had been suspended till after the festivities. She had already engaged his services for the evening in supervising the disposition of furniture in the concert and card-rooms, and the welfare of the visiting musicians.

Having made his declaration of intent, Tom took himself off for the day with his brother-in-law, in pursuit of their favourite prey, and was not seen until dinner. Fanny spent the entire morning and afternoon sending out messages to the invited houses, reviewing the condition of the reception rooms, and arranging a supplement of housemaids and footmen for the event. Since the caterers had already received their instructions, Fanny only had to send them another message reconfirming the first order, with considerable modifications, for it turned out that Tom had miscalculated the number of guests, and had forgotten all about the need for a second course. The cellars needed reviewing and renewing, transport for the musicians organised, rooms prepared for the three families who were obliged to stay overnight at Mansfield, fresh and dried flowers procured for the bouquets to be concocted by Julia – and arrangements made for a visit from a piano-tuner. Additional music and flower stands needed to be found, together with footman's wigs, billiard-room chalk and the thousand other trivia that make up the basics of a ball.

Forty-eight hours later, the essential preparations were complete, but Fanny was so weary that she began to wonder whether she would be fit to attend it. There was another problem bothering her: she had not had a moment to resolve the critical problem of what to wear. The elegance of her two relations in residence at Mansfield had highlighted the deficiency of her own wardrobe in every respect, but most notably in this one. After much hesitation, she decided to mention the problem to Mary, more to elicit sympathy than in the hope of any practical solution, for Mary's dimensions by this time were such that no loan was practicable.

Mary was extremely sympathetic.

'Fanny, you wretch, you should have spoken to me days ago; my dresser could have done wonders in making over something for you. As it is … wait – there is one possibility: an old dress of mine that was mistakenly packed in my present wardrobe. It is easily six years old, and I was much slimmer at the time, so it should fit with very few changes, and the colour will be good for you.'

Fanny thought the dress was very stylish and extravagant – though Mary assured her that it was out of date, and had originally been purchased on the Champs Elysées for a song. It fell beautifully, being an Empire dress of a heavy soft crêpe, cream in colour, with lace sleeves and a lower neckline than she had ever worn before. Though it was very comfortable, Fanny would have preferred something more conservative in style, had there been any alternative. There was none, for the pair of simple silk dresses that she usually wore for dinners and visiting were simply inadequate for the occasion. She had no option but to thank Mary and depart with the dress, but not before Mary had time to say:

'Thank me no more, it is useless to me and it is now yours.' A naughty smile crossed her face as she added: 'Are you sure that you would not like to borrow some jewellery as well – *a necklace, maybe?*'

Covered in such confusion as she scarcely thought herself capable of, Fanny shook her head and left Mary's room – telling herself that she had no time to lose in getting her aunt's dresser to effectuate some simple modifications, though she could do nothing with the neckline.

The memories associated with the necklace she had received from Mary on the occasion of the only other ball she had attended at Mansfield still had the power to disturb her. The necklace still lay somewhere at the bottom of her trinket-box, together with William's amber cross, Edmund's gold chain, and a fine string of pearls that Edmund had offered her on the occasion of the christening of their son, and which she would wear tomorrow, as her only piece of jewellery.

She was very uneasy at the continued absence of Susan, though Tom insisted that Henry knew the date of the ball and had undertaken to be there on time, especially as he had agreed to transport his sister's harp. Fanny eyed the skies apprehensively every morning and afternoon, and discovered herself listening to conversations among the servants for news on the state of the roads. By luncheon on Monday she had started to despair – acceptances from twenty families had been received for the evening, the musicians and caterers were already in the house. Mansfield wore an air of expectancy – the evening, in other words, was an assured success, but something crucial was lacking. She was convinced that the occasion would be ruined if Susan did not arrive within the next few hours.

The afternoon came and went, and Fanny completed her tasks in the reception-rooms and went upstairs to her room to dress, and still Susan had not come. Looking at her own despondent mouth in the mirror as she dressed her hair, she was finally inclined to be truthful with herself – it was not only for Susan that she had been worried these three days; she sincerely hoped that Henry Crawford had not met with any mishap on the way to Mansfield. At last she admitted to herself that she was impatient for the sight of him.

She refused to think of her mental state in any conventional romantic terms. She believed that ever since meeting him again at Everingham the fact that he had run far too often in her thoughts was due to a number of coincidental circumstances, including his astonishing kindness to her sister. She still lacked any rational explanation for this action, though sometimes the same unbidden thought came to her – that he had perhaps done it for *her*, the same Fanny, who all those years ago had unwittingly contributed to the disaster that had involved both their families. The answer that she gave herself on these occasions was always the same: she had no real reason to think such a thing.

If it was true that he had loved her sincerely thirteen years ago, it was also probably true that he had loved many others in the intervening years, and since his return home they had only met once, on her uncomfortable trip to Everingham. In retrospect, he had been polite and hospitable certainly, but neither by any reference to the past nor by any unseemly behaviour had he given her cause to think that he nourished any interesting sensations with regard to herself. In fact, she could remember how on the second morning he had vanished after breakfast, not to reappear again before their departure.

Was this the behaviour of a man in love, reunited with the object of his affections after such a long separation? Every time she considered this, Fanny was moved to annoyance at her own silliness, and resolved that their meeting again at Mansfield should be as sedate as possible – nothing in her manner should betray any agitation, or the untoward interest he had started to arouse in her. She was convinced that meeting him again would restore her to normality – she would herself see how senseless and divorced from reality her thinking had become, and she would meet him calmly, as befits an old acquaintance. Adjusting the pearl necklace around her neck, she viewed herself in the mirror. She looked well, except that her face wanted colour. The dress fell gracefully, and the regrettable neckline looked very becoming, even to her own critical eye.

A persistent knocking on the lower half of the door announced the determined presence of her son, come to view his parent and say goodnight, for he and his cousins had permission for a special treat that night. They were to feast on a late supper in the nursery, and then watch the proceedings from the gallery before going to bed.

'Mama, you look like that lady in the story – the one who was married to the magician. Can Maria stay up with us till eleven o'clock? Manners said that she would have to go to bed by nine, but you know that the dancing cannot start till at least ten – '

Fanny smoothed back his hair. 'Since when have you been so interested in dancing, my son?'

'Mr Tilly says that it is part of a gentleman's accomplishments.'

'What, is Mr Tilly a good dancer?'

'He says not, but I think he must be, and he plans to dance the first two with aunt Susan, so we *must* all be present, Mama – '

Fanny heaved a sigh. 'Well, dearest, Susan will have to dance with Mr Tilly on some other occasion. She is probably on the London road somewhere, putting up at an inn for the night.'

Edmund looked puzzled. 'But mama, it was aunt Susan who sent me to ask you whether Maria could stay up with us, as aunt Julia's maid said that she couldn't, and Maria cried so hard we thought she would be sick. Then Manners said – '

His mother interrupted him hurriedly – 'Susan is here? When did she arrive?'

'Soon after tea. She and Major Crawford got stuck once on the road outside Leicester, and had to wait for a wheel-change, but aunt Susan says it was a comfortable journey and she plans to dance all night, for it is her first ball!'

His mother needed some moments to digest this information. Kissing him fondly, she gave him the permission he sought, and then sat listening to his rejoicing voice as it departed down the corridor. Turning to the mirror once more, she could see that her face no longer lacked colour.

But for some reason she was reluctant to leave her room, and kept on finding reasons for delaying the moment of going downstairs, although she had a dozen details to check there before the guests started to arrive. She needed some toilet-water, another handkerchief, a change of gloves, and then discovered that she had misplaced her wedding-ring, which cost her several minutes of searching. Twenty minutes later she accepted the inevitable, and shutting the door of her room was turning to go downstairs when she almost ran into Henry Crawford, coming from his room and hurrying downstairs by the same way.

They stood together on the main landing, looking at each other, and for a long moment it was as if they had never seen each other before. Then they reached out and shook hands solemnly, still looking each into the other's face. At last Fanny smiled.

'Welcome to Mansfield.'

Henry answered her smile slowly, bowing an instant over her hand before releasing it. 'I am glad to be here at last. Have you seen Susan as yet?'

'No, I have only just learned of your – I mean her arrival here. It was so kind of you … ' Her voice petered off lamely, as she started to remember the extent of his kindness. She felt a wave of warm colour rising up from her inadequate neckline, the more so as Henry's eyes had dropped to her necklace for a moment before returning to her face.

He smiled once more, this time with his eyes as well as his mouth: 'You look very beautiful this evening, Mrs Bertram. Let us join the others downstairs.'

There was no polite way of refusing the proffered arm, Fanny thought confusedly as they slowly descended the main staircase and made to enter the drawing-room.

17

*T*hey were delayed for a moment at the door, where Baddeley's imposing form blocked any further advance, until he had smiled at Major Crawford and bowed a welcome to Mansfield. Immediately inside the drawing-room, Henry was pounced on by his sister, all smiles and trills of happy laughter:

'Dear Henry! how good of you to be ready on time! I hear from Tom that you had some problems at Leicester?'

'Just outside Leicester, actually, otherwise we would have been here this morning.'

'And many thanks for thinking to bring my hairdresser. I have been missing her services dreadfully.'

'I had need of someone to chaperone Susan, and Browne seemed keen to accompany us. You look extremely fine,' looking at his sister critically, 'are those earrings new?'

'A trifle Tom bought me in Rome – I think they are Venetian in design. Well, Fanny – as I thought, the dress fits you very well, and the pearls are just right.'

Poor Fanny endured once more the sensation of two pairs of eyes fixed on her necklace, before Mary Bertram walked away with her brother, to allow him to pay his respects to her mother-in-law.

Fanny was interested enough to observe this meeting, particularly as Julia Yates had just joined the group. She stood watching as Henry bowed over the older woman's hand, courteously listening to what was evidently a speech of thanks for having brought Susan home. Watching his face light up as he smiled, Fanny found herself wondering how she had ever failed to think him handsome. The word was perhaps ill-chosen, he was more accurately described as 'charming', since his attractiveness lay in the intelligence and comprehension of his regard rather than in any regularity of feature or form.

He then turned to Julia. Fanny saw him bend his dark head over her hand, and saw her simper over his next remark. She believed rather than felt that Julia looked extremely elegant, her robe was of some sumptuous material, and looked well-designed – but to Fanny's inexperienced eye it looked remarkably similar to two other dresses she had already seen her cousin wear. In addition to her new gown, Julia wore her mother's ruby and diamond set, and Fanny saw Mary's considering glance upon them before she turned away to answer a remark from her husband.

Fanny scanned the room for her sister: 'Susan – oh, Susan!' This was said with a warm handclasp, followed by the kindest embrace.

'Fanny – I almost didn't recognise you, you look so beautiful.'

'Susan, we have so much to talk about. Save some time for me later – I must see to the rooms – '

She had time only for this brief exchange with Susan before hurrying away to the ball-room, where several details remained to be seen to. Susan looked particularly happy this evening, a return to her gay and smiling self, and was very becomingly dressed, though Fanny did not have the time to comment upon this before running away, her head full of card-packs and candlesticks.

In the event, it was as well that she had left an hour for these last-minute preparations, for they took somewhat longer. One of the violins had been damaged in travelling and could not be used, necessitating a change in programme and a search for some other music, which could not be located in the music-room but which Stephen found in the library. Madame Alberti, the principal singer, was threatening a cold, and needed more shawls as well as a rather large hot drink liberally laced with brandy. At the insistence of the pianist, the position of the piano needed to be changed, and one of Julia's tasteful bouquets placed upon it consequently dislodged, which meant a hunt for another flower-stand.

A few more of such eventualities in the other reception rooms, and all was ready. Fortunately, by now Susan had joined her, and in addition to her stalwart help, the sisters were able to rapidly discuss the situation in Portsmouth. But not for long, for from the sounds in the hall and on the carriage-way, most of the guests had arrived, and these were already assembled when Fanny finally re-entered the concert-room, where proceedings were already more than a quarter of an hour overdue. Tom was making a brief speech of welcome as she entered, looking about her in vain for an empty seat. Finally, she saw one in the second row, and hesitantly took it, much disliking being seated so far into the front of the audience.

The concert was so planned to give the professional musicians an opportunity to perform during the first part of the programme, which consisted of several Italian and French songs followed by some madrigals accompanied on the piano and violin. Fanny had attended a few concerts of this sort during her marriage – this being Edmund's favourite sort of music – which she did not appreciate to the same extent, considering it rather as music that provided a background to thought, since it did not require much concentration. As the songs succeeded each other, she found herself relaxing, and even observing her neighbours, several of whom she was acquainted with from past visits to Mansfield.

At the end of a particularly sugary love-duet, the nervous young man seated on her left leaned over to ask her something about the next song. Turning her head to answer him, she saw out of the corner of her eye that Henry was seated almost behind her, two chairs to the left, and she blushed when she saw that he was watching her. He was leaning back in his chair, looking bored and speculative rather than rapt in the music, and upon catching her eye he did not turn his gaze elsewhere, but continued looking straight at her. Somewhat awkwardly, she turned to answer her neighbour, being careful not to look to the left again, though several times she imagined she felt Henry's glance on her, at moments when her cheek or shoulder burned.

The first part of the concert was followed by an interval of several minutes, during which the guests moved about, gossiped and changed their seats. Fanny would have liked a seat somewhere at the back, but though she actually stood up and looked about her, she could not see an empty chair in the desired area. Henry's seat behind her was vacant when the second part of the concert began, and at first she felt relieved, thinking that she would be spared the embarrassment of the past half-hour, but presently she knew from the sensation of being watched once more, that he had not absconded, but was probably seated somewhere at the rear of the room.

The second part of the programme afforded the guests an opportunity to participate, and several people had already given notice of intention to sing or play. Tom himself volunteered a folk-song, accompanied by his wife on the piano; who then moved to the harp, amidst much applause, to accompany Julia's Irish song. Stephen proved to have a very pleasant tenor singing voice, and Dr Thwaite came up, somewhat unexpectedly, with a wobbly bass 'meditation' before some Christmas songs gave way to the country music that concluded the concert and set the mood for the opening of the ball.

As the company moved towards the ball-room amidst laughter, congratulation and fan-waving, Fanny looked around for Henry. He was not seated, but was standing against the wall on the far side of the room, in conversation with a dark-haired woman who was seated just in front of him. She had half-expected that he would approach to talk to her, but he did not, and instead she found herself in conversation with Tom, who immediately asked her to dance.

'Not the first two, Fanny, for I must open the ball with Mary, but keep any two for me later on. What do you say to the after-supper dances, if you do not object to a waltz? Good – ' and he walked rapidly away to where the musicians were reassembling their forces for the second phase of the evening.

Fanny moved to the card-room. She had declined to dance for the first half-hour, being occupied with settling the card-players and chaperons to everyone's satisfaction. She was promised to Stephen for the two next dances, and when she re-entered the ball-room he was waiting for her, in conversation with his uncle, who immediately solicited her hand for the two following dances. A little surprised, but with no reason for refusing, she accepted, and watched him walk away before allowing Stephen to lead her into the set, in which she noticed that Henry was partnering the dark-haired lady she had noticed earlier.

It is written somewhere that the best way of inducing a headache is to do what one does not want to do, while at the same time not doing what one really wants to do. Fanny was able to test the veracity of this observation during her dances with Stephen, who, although as amiable as ever, spoke for the entire half-hour of his joy at seeing Susan again, and of her delightful qualities. Much as she sympathised with him, and much as she generally agreed with his main premise, for the first time she found him slightly tedious. Yet the moment of her release from his company brought no relief, for it heralded the arrival of his beaming uncle, and the prospect of another half-hour of effort during the country-dances, maintaining a smiling face, and trying to concentrate on his conversation.

Dr Thwaite's discourse kept pace with his bodily movements; he changed topics as rapidly as the figures changed in the square, but every topic was related to the great subject of Matrimony. He commenced with Susan and Stephen – they seemed well-suited – fortunate in every respect except that of material prosperity – had much to look forward to in the joys of the married state – these not necessarily restricted to the very young – perhaps more profoundly felt in the maturer individual – a second marriage often happier than the first – every person's duty to marry if they can and produce children – a child's need of a parent, two parents, a multiplicity of parents?

At some stage of her deepening headache Fanny wondered how she and Dr Thwaite had got to be talking about her son, but so voluble was the good doctor that she had no chance of placing any words, contenting herself with assisting his statements with nods and smiles. There was an awkward moment during the dance when she looked across the room to where Mary Bertram danced with her brother, and caught the lady's insinuating smile, before she turned to Henry and whispered something behind her fan.

At the end of their dances, her partner seemed decided to take Fanny into supper, but this she firmly declined, pleading a number of things to do, not the least of which was to look in on the children upstairs, as she had promised. Although it was past eleven o'clock, she was not hungry, and thought that a few moments of rest in the quiet of her room might dissipate her headache. It was unfortunate, therefore, that as she reached the bend in the staircase and looked down on the company moving into the supper-room, she saw Mary and Tom leading in, followed by Henry with his dark-haired acquaintance on his arm.

As she expected, the children were already fast asleep, in despite of their late permission, though Edmund's sticky fingers and crumb-strewn coverlet bore mute evidence of belated forbidden pleasures. In the girls' room, Maria clutched her doll, her thumb in her mouth, while Jane lay as one laid out for burial, an image of rectitude, even in sleep. Fanny smiled in despite of her headache as she made her way to her room. Here she drank a glass of water and rested in the cosy darkness for a quarter of an hour before deciding to make some repairs to her hair.

As she did so, she was struck by the expression of dissatisfaction about her eyes and mouth – she wore the look of a disappointed child who has been promised a treat that has not materialised. She had not the time to inquire into the reason for this thought, for as she patted her head and moved to straighten her necklace before turning away from the mirror, it snapped in her hand, spilling the glowing beads on to the floor at her feet.

Aghast, she sat for several moments in the candle-light. She had nothing suitable to replace it, and must return to the ball, if at all, without any jewellery. Suddenly she felt close to tears, and were it not for the dances she had promised to Tom, she would probably have decided against returning to the ball-room for the moment. But even as she debated the possibility, stooping to collect as many of the pearls as she could discover in the semi-darkness, she heard the violins strike up the waltz, and knew she should go downstairs.

The first person she saw on entering the ball-room was Henry Crawford, who came up to her with a message from Tom.

'During supper he became involved with Charles Maddox and a group of serious card-players, and I fear his plans for the rest of the evening do not include dancing. He sends you his apologies, and has delegated me to stand in for his dances with you.'

Fanny was both embarrassed at her cousin's coolness and relieved that he had not been kept waiting for her.

'This is too much, to expect you to pay his social debts! If you do not mind, I would rather sit this one out with my aunt, for I know she plans to retire early,' and was turning away when Henry placed a hand on her arm.

'If you have no objection, Mrs Bertram, I would above all things desire to dance these waltzes with you. Shall we?'

115

18

*A*nyone who at first observed Mrs Edmund Bertram waltzing with Major Crawford at the Mansfield Christmas ball might have been forgiven for thinking that they were not very well acquainted – for the first ten minutes not a word was exchanged. Though outwardly calm enough, Fanny kept her eyes cast down in an effort to still the knocking of her heart in her chest, and between that and the need to concentrate on her steps there was at first no possibility of conversation.

Henry was possibly regretting the copiousness of the Mansfield cellars at supper – for this or for some other reason he was having trouble with his own breathing. Since he did not need to concentrate on his steps, however, he eventually decided to speak, and started rather stiltedly:

'You dance delightfully – have you waltzed often before?'

After an instant's pause her eyes lifted. 'No, never before – I learned the steps with Susan, last year.'

She did not detail the fact that it had taken the pair of them several hours to master the technique. But there was a vast difference between solitary gyrations with Susan in the dim nursery, and being here in the lighted ball-room thronged with spectators, moving within the circle of Henry's arm, turning and twirling with his face so close to hers that his breath moved upon her cheek.

Henry persisted with the topic, in an attempt to make her look up at him again:

'It is now very popular in London, but I can remember that before I left for India it was quite unknown – I hear that until a few years ago it was considered very "fast", and that one actually needed special permission to waltz at Almacks!'

The reference to the time before he left for India was a mistake, for she did not look up again for several minutes, and he watched the stain rise from her neck to her hairline before deciding to make another effort.

'This evening promises to be the success of the Mansfield season. Do you know how many people are present?'

She glanced up rapidly, before looking away over his shoulder. 'Close to seventy guests, I think, but almost twenty were non-dancers, and are occupied in the card-room or elsewhere. It is nothing to Mary's reception in London, of course.'

He shrugged: 'That was an intolerable crush, to my sister's great delight.'

Once more she looked at him. 'Poor Mary, she must have been completely exhausted – no wonder she was unwell as a result.'

Henry looked amused. 'Is that what she wrote to you? The truth is, she hired someone to organise the entire event for her, and I can guarantee that it cost her very little personal effort, though I imagine it was expensive.' Sufficiently encouraged to change topics, Henry found one easily. In a low, confidential tone he inquired: 'Has something happened to your necklace?'

There was a noticeable hesitation, and she stumbled slightly before answering softly: 'The string broke, just now, upstairs in my room.'

Henry guessed that it had been a gift from her husband, and remembered the sentimental value that Fanny was used to attach to such objects. He was at the same time remembering something else: the force of her regard, and how it spoke to him, loaded with reproach and significance. Feeling slightly dazed, he could think of nothing to say except somewhat lamely: 'It can probably be restrung. There must be a service in a jeweller's shop in Nottingham or Northampton, or someone could take it to London for you.'

While his mind ran on to the possibilities for future communication this eventually opened up, she omitted to mention that she had worn it regularly for almost nine years, and had already decided to have it reset and offer it to Susan as a present. But once she remembered Susan, there was at last a topic she could safely initiate.

'I feel I must thank you sincerely for bringing Susan back to us in time for Christmas – we were really glad to see her – '

117

Henry smiled more broadly. 'And is that the reason why you professed yourself so happy to see me this evening? I had been hoping for a welcome on my own account!'

Fanny smiled anxiously: 'I think you cannot be serious? You must know how very pleased we all were to see you at Mansfield today – I merely wished to thank you for the special favour in bringing back Susan – '

Henry interrupted: 'It may be preferable to leave your thanks for another occasion when we have time to talk at length. This is a ball, and our business is to be dancing!' His teasing smile robbed the words of any sting, and for the first time Fanny found herself relaxing, able to forget her steps and the spectators, and move simply in enjoyment with the music. Your casual observer at this point would have reached a very different conclusion about their relationship, particularly if he had noticed the way the gentleman's arm tightened about the lady, and the way she smiled shyly at him as the steps of the dance drew them together.

Alas, the slowing of the music signalled the end of the first dance – the couples separated and took a short turn about the room while the musicians tuned up for the second. Fanny was so flushed, probably from her exertions, that she needed to use her fan, and was busily employed with it as they passed two ladies in conversation, idly watching the dancing. It was her aunt and one of her friends, Mrs Oliver, and she heard the former say:

'Yes, isn't it a wonderful success! But then you cannot imagine how much time and effort poor Tom put into it – I had no idea he was so devoted.'

Henry raised an eyebrow at Fanny. She could read his thoughts with a fair degree of accuracy, and he did not really need to say: 'Yes, I think I know exactly how much work poor Tom managed to put into it – I imagine the sum total of his efforts was a guest list and a command to the caterers.'

Fanny was startled at his perceptiveness: 'I think you are not quite fair to my cousin. He meant very well – '

'I know Tom quite well enough, and I know my own sister even better. I think that you probably did most of the work for this evening, as I cannot imagine Lady Bertram doing very much to help.'

Fanny had not often experienced this pleasant assurance that someone somewhere was unconditionally prejudiced in her favour, no matter what the circumstances. But a sense of fairness forced her to persist:

'Julia did the flower arrangements – '

'Julia! I expect she had very little time to spare from her own toilette.' His light tone changed to one of seriousness: 'It is a pity to see a fine girl such as Julia used to be reduced to a fashion figurine. What are her children like?'

'Jane is very like what Julia used to be as a child. I prefer Maria, perhaps because she is the bosom-bow of my own son.'

'Was Edmund the young man who came up the driveway as we arrived? He has a critical eye for a horse, and is very full of questions.'

Fanny frowned slightly. 'I hope he did not annoy you? He is horse-mad at the moment, ever since Stephen Tilly started teaching him to ride.'

Henry laughed. 'You need not worry about him annoying me – on the contrary, he seemed an interesting child, and I was crafty enough to hand him over to Ahmed after a few minutes; no man alive knows more about a horse!'

At the start of the second dance they were both more relaxed, and relieved at how easy light conversation had proved to be between them. Fanny blushed less and smiled more, looking directly at him as they conversed. He seemed interested in Edmund, and asked her several questions about him, and also about Stephen. He did not mention Betsey, but had nothing but appreciation for Susan's 'sense, buoyancy and energy – Tilly is a fortunate young man indeed'.

'Sense is Susan's strongest quality,' Fanny agreed.

Henry sensed a certain slight reserve in her voice. 'You seem to find something lacking – do you think sensibility more important than sense?'

'No indeed, in fact I know from experience – ' Here Fanny stopped, finding herself in danger of revealing more than was warranted in the space of a dance.

Henry waited in some suspense for her to continue. When she did not, he took up the conversation once again:

'Do you not find it dangerous to categorise people as being either sensitive or sensible, for example? Is it not rather true to say that we are all capable of a range of behaviours, depending upon each separate situation?'

Fanny hesitated once more. 'But on the whole, people do tend to fall into types, and typical behaviour can surely be predicted in many cases ... it all depends upon how well one knows a person.'

'Say rather, upon how well one *thinks* one knows a person! But is it really possible to *know* anyone completely? For example, you think you know me, but what do you *really know* about me?' His voice suddenly sounded very earnest.

Although Fanny was disturbed by the change in the level of the conversation from the theoretical to the personal, and was consequently afraid to look directly at him, she found the courage to reply:

'I know that you are in many ways a very generous person – '

Henry spoke rapidly and passionately: 'You *know nothing* of me – almost all your information is encompassed by my behaviour during an idle summer thirteen years ago!'

The music was drawing to a close, their steps were becoming slower. There was an uncomfortable silence of some length before he continued speaking, in a calmer tone: 'I have pretensions to a somewhat better knowledge of your character – I still think of you as one of those fortunate people that seem to unite every good quality in their person.'

At this, Fanny experienced much less embarrassment than one would have thought. Not even his reference to the distant summer could disturb her as much as could be expected, for she was once more conscious only of the strong undercurrent of pleasure at being in the company of someone who placed an exaggerated value on one's character and person.

She was far less aware by this time of the other people present, and it was not until the second dance was nearly over that she looked away for an instant from Henry into Julia's suspicious face as it floated past, and remembered, as her aunt Norris used to say, '*who she was, and where she was.*'

John Yates had noted with some satisfaction how pleased Fanny and the Major seemed to be with each other, and lost no time in scoring off his wife. 'What did I say, m'dear? Thwaite stands nowhere, that's what I maintain!'

He did not understand why his wife seemed so furious at this mild observation, nor why she was obviously keeping as sharp an eye on Fanny as was consistent with her stylish air. John Yates was not a clever man, but even the cleverest of men are often as infants in the ways of women.

At the end of their dances, Henry had obtained from Fanny the information that she had not supped as yet, and insisted on seating her in a corner of the card-room while he went foraging for something to eat. She sat in reflective silence for several minutes, before realising that she could overhear the conversation from a nearby table, where four ladies consulted their cards and assassinated characters at the same time.

They were discussing someone who had just married a very rich older woman to save himself from bankruptcy, 'for it seems, my dear, that Sotherton was mortgaged to the hilt, both his previous wives having been very spendthrift!'

'Nonsense, *ma chère*, he was married to the first for less than a year. In fact,' looking about before continuing, 'actually, she was – '

A lot of fan waving and tittering followed, and consequently Fanny lost most of the exchange, till she caught the tail end of a sentence: 'with none other than the eldest daughter of the house!' There was a pause of several seconds before the same lady continued speaking, and at last Fanny was able to catch: 'and such an air! It is no wonder he has the Devil's own reputation with women, if the latest from my god-daughter in London is anything to go by.'

'And did the latest – I presume your source is Mrs Nevers – disclose anything material as to the size of his fortune? That is surely more *à propos* than digging up past scandals, no matter who was involved!'

Another voice interrupted: 'It is certain that he made an immense fortune while in the service of the Company. My niece Pamela had it from a cousin of the Skinner's, in whose circle he moved in Delhi after he left Calcutta – and we know that her husband is still out there, so she should be well informed.'

'Is not Pamela here tonight? I thought I saw her dancing earlier this evening, with the gallant Major.'

'Indeed you did – and she said that during supper he subjected her to a litany of questions on her husband's career and future prospects – it seems he plans to set up in business with him and with a few other old India hands, as soon as he gets back. She gave it to me as her opinion that he is rather *épris* – ' here the speaker looked around and discovered Fanny seated within her auditory circle. She lowered her voice as a result, and Fanny lost the rest of the conversation.

Henry returned soon afterwards with a plate of creamed chicken and two glasses of champagne. Unaware of the avid curiosity of the nearby card-table, he found Fanny once more a monosyllabic companion, and one who moreover was resolute in her refusal to dance again. She decided to bear her aunt company till that lady retired, and after that to sit beside Mary, who was looking rather fagged, and was obviously waiting impatiently for the last guests to depart.

Fanny was obliged to dance one last time, however, with Tom, who returned from the card-room flushed with success, and was determined to enliven the evening for his little cousin – perhaps by way of thanking her for her invaluable aid in helping him to organise the ball. Taking permission from his yawning wife, he carried Fanny into the set against her protests, and delivered the *coup de grâce* by treading heavily on her foot. His aggrieved complaints at her clumsiness lasted till the ball was over.

Though Fanny limped through the rest of the evening, it was almost two hours later before the last carriage departed, and she could seek at last the quiet of her room. After a day of so much excitement, it is the lot of a heroine to spend a sleepless night. I regret to report that Fanny was so far unaware of her duty in this respect as to fall asleep as soon as her head touched the pillow. True, one may make all sorts of excuses for her, but the sad fact remains that she had every reason to lie awake thinking of someone who was perhaps lying awake thinking of her, and that she wasted the opportunity of doing so.

19

*F*anny was able to recoup this loss almost immediately, for the mere fact of falling asleep at past three o'clock in the morning after a long and tiring day is no guarantee of an extended sleep next morning. Our heroine found herself awake at her usual hour, and since a somewhat later breakfast than usual had been ordered, she had nearly two hours in which to lie abed, thinking about the person she had omitted to dream about the night before.

It was necessary to devote some time to the examination of Henry Crawford, and particularly to her own state of mind with regard to him. She had as yet no notion of imagining herself in love, but she was forced to admit that at present she viewed him in a very different light from what she had in the past, when her attitude had been marked by an ingrained prejudice that had kept her from any objective appraisal of his character.

'Circumstances alter cases', as Lady Bertram was in the habit of saying, but in this case it was not only the circumstances that had changed, but the individuals themselves. Both she and Henry had altered, and it was to be hoped that the mistakes of the past were behind them now. When she looked back at herself at eighteen, she seemed an unbearably priggish miss, quite incapable of seeing Henry as other than as a trifler. She hoped that she had gained some experience of life and had been tempered by grief; just as, with the years, Henry seemed to have acquired depth and seriousness of purpose. She admitted to herself that he was an interesting and agreeable companion, and seemed well-disposed towards the Bertrams in general, in despite of the past. Here Fanny was obliged to remind herself that this was only to be expected, for in despite of mitigating circumstances he had to share responsibility with Maria for the disastrous events of Easter 1809.

In what lay his attractiveness to women? Last night had served to remind her of the effect he exerted at times on some women of her acquaintance, and potentially – as witnessed by the events of the ball – even on herself.

But why – and here she was obliged to slow down the pace of her thoughts – why must the attractiveness of an individual immediately have repercussions on his or her neighbour? May one not appreciate the desirable qualities in one or another of one's acquaintance without thereby wishing for a somewhat deeper relationship with that person? And what if what she had imagined at some moments of the evening was true – that Henry Crawford still felt something of his old interest in her? What if he renewed his courtship of her after all these years? Here Fanny had to pause once more for several moments and try to control her thoughts. It was not only someone's lazy smile and the warmth of a regard, or the tone of a voice, that mattered, when a life-long relationship was under consideration.

Fanny reminded herself that she was a widow with a very small income and a child at her charge. She could ill afford to place her future in the care of someone who might prove unreliable, and whose eventual unfaithfulness might incur greater unhappiness than she had ever experienced in the haven of security that was Mansfield. Was not peace, quiet and stasis preferable to passion, hectic excitement and movement? Recalling some moments during the ball, she felt a profound mistrust of her own reactions, as dangerously irrational.

If she had the choice, would she choose Mansfield or Everingham? Would she ever have the choice? What part of his attentions were the result of her fevered imaginings, and what part came from that general gallantry towards women that she had observed in him long ago?

Fanny eventually arose, to no better conclusion than that she should be more cautious in her relations with Henry Crawford than ever before. With this in mind she went downstairs to breakfast, where the first person she met was the subject of her morning reflections, and they had at least ten minutes to discuss the weather and the events of the coming day before being joined by the Hon. John Yates, still in search of a companion for the day's sport, and doomed to disappointment with Henry.

'I'm afraid that I have had more than my fair share of shooting at people and animals in the past ten years.'

John Yates' interest was fairly caught.

'Were you in the habit of hunting regularly in India?'

'No. In fact, after my first experience of a tiger-hunt, I am pleased to say that I never attended another.'

'Why was that?'

'The tally for the day was five tigers – one beater mauled to death, one elephant disembowelled, and someone whose name I forget lost an eye and the use of his left arm.'

There was a short silence before Yates spoke again: 'But surely other animals – deer, for example?'

'India is full of animals. Several variety of gazelle could be seen in the region around Mehwat, and we had to shoot them regularly for food. Otherwise, we shot at brigands, buffalo, bear and crocodile, probably in that order.'

Edmund had come into the dining room during the last part of the conversation, and now approached Henry with reverence. Pleased perhaps to change the topic, Henry turned to him:

'Hello, young man! Is that a cat I see peeping out of your pocket – why is he riding there?'

'Because he is not allowed to run around downstairs when Pug is about, sir.'

'And why is that?'

Edmund's tone was confidential: 'Because he doesn't know how to behave,' with a reflective glance at Fanny, 'perhaps his mother never taught him.'

'What about his father?'

The answer was definitive. 'He doesn't have a father,' to which Henry merely smiled.

Edmund had come to solicit the company of his mother on a walk later that morning, and Fanny rapidly agreed – to avoid a debate before the expanding company, though with strong mental reservations. She had to remain in the breakfast-room rather longer than the others, for two of the three families who had passed the night at Mansfield would be departing after that meal. The Hunstons, a rather older couple, and their son – a spotty youth of nineteen who had been Fanny's neighbour at the concert – were invited to spend Christmas at Mansfield. Robert Hunston, in despite of his complexion, showed his good taste by an inclination to admire Fanny, which he manifested by a determination to remain in her company for the rest of the morning.

After bidding a hearty farewell to his visitors, Tom disappeared for the rest of the day with John Yates, and since no other lady (except Susan, who was interviewing Manners on the subject of the next day's Christmas dinner) had appeared downstairs as yet, Fanny completed supervising the clearing operations after the ball before ceding to Edmund's request for a walk. She had not yet seen Stephen, and had it in mind that she would shelve the outing off on to him, but it appeared that he and Susan had urgent business in the village, whence they had departed in the trap by mid-morning. Henry had gone out in the curricle, so just before mid-day Fanny had no other option than to set out for her walk with Edmund and the assiduous Robert as her companions.

The woods afforded them their usual welcome, though they did not see more than two jackdaws, and spent fifteen minutes waiting beside a badger's hole, where Edmund maintained he had glimpsed a movement. Probably from jealousy, Edmund held on to his mother's hand as he had not done for several years, and interrupted every attempt of Robert's at conversation with a counter-question of his own. Torn between annoyance and amusement, Fanny did not find her usual pleasure in the outing, neither was she in the mood to admire the winter sunshine and the deep shadows on the barks and the frosty ground.

They walked further than they intended, and had just turned about for the return to the house, when they glimpsed the curricle coming towards them along the road between the trees. Interrupting a somewhat rambling story of Robert's, Fanny had smiled and waved before she realised that her gesture could be misconstrued. Shouting with joy, Edmund ran up to meet the equipage, while Henry climbed down and walked over to meet them. As he walked back to the vehicle with her, he told her that he had been to the inn, four miles off, to collect a horse that he had left there for shoeing the previous day. Fanny did not understand why he had brought his curricle to Mansfield in addition to his carriage, till, with a smile, he explained the need for a mode of transportation for his sister's harp.

Robert and Edmund had already reached the curricle, and for the first time that morning showed some accord in their admiration of the horses, and in the questions they put to Ahmed, a thin dark man who sat holding the reins and grinning down at them as he attempted to answer them, in strongly accented guttural speech. Henry and Fanny stood by patiently for some minutes while the requisitory continued, until Ahmed turned and spoke to Henry in his own tongue, who immediately translated for Fanny:

'He suggests taking the young gentlemen back in the curricle, if you have no objection to walking home with me?'

Fanny did no more than nod, and Ahmed added something which made Henry laugh as he helped Edmund up to his seat, squeezed between the other two. Though obviously disconcerted at thus leaving the field to a rival, Robert could not disguise his pleasure at actually holding the reins for the first part of the journey. As she watched the curricle receding, Fanny was not aware of any undue shyness, merely some regret that their walk back home would not take more than half an hour at the utmost, whereas a few minutes ago she had been regretting the length of it.

'I envy you the joy you have of Edmund,' he was saying as they moved forwards, 'and not only of Edmund – the atmosphere at Mansfield is still that of a family house. It is what I never had, even as a child, and what perhaps Mary and myself lacked the most.'

Fanny demurred gently: 'Mansfield has always been a family house, but that in itself is insufficient to give it interest. At the present season you see it full of life – most of the time it is excessively quiet, even dull.'

He turned to look at her. 'Do you regret having had only one child – is Edmund lonely?'

'It is true that he is a solitary child. There are no companions of his age at the house.'

Henry was still looking at her. 'Do you still enjoy living at Mansfield after all these years?'

This was a difficult question to answer simply, and Fanny hesitated before answering slowly: 'I think having a family gives one a sense of purpose. I cannot imagine what my life would be without it.'

He had turned away, and was looking through the trees towards the white silhouette of the house, situated beyond the next rise. 'It is what I want – above everything – at present,' he said.

There was a somewhat intense pause before he changed the subject by asking her whether she had news from Portsmouth. This reminded her that she had not as yet thanked him in person for his kindness to Betsey, and she directly embarked on a speech of thanks, nonetheless heartfelt for being somewhat confused in presentation, which he cut short before she was halfway done.

'Did your mother mention Richard Upton?'

'Yes, indeed. It seems that he has developed a spirit of controversy which she thinks decreases his chances with my sister.'

Henry laughed outright. 'He is following my advice in the matter. Betsey is like Maria in more ways than one, and she needs opposition to sustain her interest. If he perseveres, I wager they will be married by Easter.'

Fanny could not help smiling, her peace hardly ruffled by the reference to Maria. It was somewhere near here that her fallen tree lay, with the torn page from Maria's diary strewn about in the leaves beneath it. The memory of those days, like the souvenir of Maria herself, seemed to have receded – and she had no time to reflect upon this phenomenon, for Henry was speaking once more:

'William seemed very concerned about your mother, in case she may have to live entirely alone in future, with the departure of her maid – the one with the Biblical name I cannot recall; was it Ruth or Rachel?'

Fanny laughed. 'It is Rebecca, and she has lived with my mother for fourteen years, but is soon to wed and change residence. I hope that when Lady Bertram solves her problem of where to live in future, she will make a place for my mother with her, as Susan's marriage will mean that my aunt will otherwise be entirely alone with me.'

He was looking at her intently. 'Do you want to spend the rest of your life waiting upon your aunt?'

There was another intense silence, which Fanny in something of a panic hurried to break. 'I should be pleased to spend most of my time with her, though I have some plans for making a few short journeys in the new year.'

Henry's tone was speculative: 'It is an excellent idea – to house the two sisters together; one cannot help being struck by how much they have in common.' After a short pause he continued: 'Where do you mean to travel to?'

Fanny found herself talking quite easily of a few of her future plans, especially those concerning her projected visit to London and William. Henry was full of advice, and having ascertained that she had seen nothing of consequence on her previous trips to the metropolis, had this to say:

'There is a great deal more to London than that! You must let Mary look after you properly – which, as she is no longer feeling sick most of the time, she will be delighted to do.'

Their conversation was so agreeable to her, so strongly imbued with a sense of freedom, that they were almost in the driveway before she remembered her resolve of only that morning. Releasing his arm, she turned away from her companion, and quickened her steps till they were in the hall. As they entered the morning-room she saw that the rest of the family and their guests were gathered around a cold luncheon, and it greatly increased her unease to realise that nearly every eye was turned upon the pair of them in speculation.

20

*T*his embarrassing state of affairs was in no way improved when Julia called out to her across the room: 'Fanny, where can you have been walking to? Edmund and Robert were home quite half an hour ago! You look almost hectic, and I noticed that you did not look well last night at the ball, either – are you sure that you are not sickening for something?'

Fanny needed to exert some control in order to ignore the solicitude of her cousin and start a gentle conversation with Stephen about his errand to the village.

Edmund and Robert had evidently been talking about Henry's wonderful equipage, for Mr Hunston, a gentlemanlike man, approached Henry and began a short exchange on horseflesh, ending with the observation that he was fortunate indeed – in Ahmed – to have lured away to England such an expert on the subject.

Henry snorted with laughter. 'I assure you that I never attempted to lure him anywhere – quite the opposite!'

Mr Hunston looked inquiringly, and Henry explained: 'His family was butchered before his eyes and I had the misfortune to save his life, whence he simply transferred his allegiance to me. It will be impossible to rid myself of him for the rest of his days.'

Mr Hunston responded with a courteous bow: 'Well, at least you can claim to have gained one good thing from your stay in India.'

Henry's expression sobered. 'I doubt it is possible to live for any considerable length of time in India without gaining and losing several things. I was one of the fortunate ones, in that I gained what I lacked at that stage of my life.'

'And what was that, may I ask?'

'A sense of purpose, seeing that I had the time to review some of my larger aims.'

'And was that all?'

'By no means – I also gained a second and larger fortune than I had before.'

His sister interrupted, from across the room: 'And is that not a good thing? Why Henry, you sound quite stuffy – this is what comes of walking with Fanny before luncheon!'

Mr Hunston politely ignored the interruption. 'What did you lose, if you do not mind telling us?'

'Something of my youth and easy temperament, and – what will probably prove dearer – a considerable portion of my good health. I am regularly visited by a debilitating fever, which a doctor over there told me is very common, and may take anything up to ten years to work itself out of my system, if at all.'

Mr Hunston looked concerned, and moving closer to Henry, continued on the subject in a low voice. Fanny had looked up from her conversation with Stephen to catch most of this exchange, before moving to join Mary and Julia, who seemed engaged in an absorbing conversation at the far end of the room. As she grew nearer, she caught the end of Mary's speech:

'If by *nicer* you mean more attractive, that is easily explained. He is certainly older, but in a man that does not signify. He is very much richer, still unmarried but with a definite penchant for the married state. What more could one hope for?'

Julia's answer came at once: 'That he choose a suitable wife, and marry soon.'

Mary tossed her curls before speaking. 'So desperate was the chase for him in London that some of my friends wagered that he would not last the season. But I think that this time he will be *nicer* in the sense of more particular, and take the trouble to find *chaussure à son pied!*'

Julia looked slightly confused: 'No, by nicer I meant somehow gentler, *kinder* than I can remember him.'

Mary laughed outright at this. 'That I take leave to doubt! If he appears gentler and kinder, beware the wolf in sheep's clothing – he may be playing some deep game.'

131

Fanny was still meditating on this last remark when she came downstairs to dinner some hours later and saw a letter on the hall table addressed to her. She noted that it had come from the Parsonage, and thinking it might contain some detail of the next day's services, she put it into her pocket to look at later, for Baddeley had already rung the dinner-bell, and the move towards the dining-room had started.

The master of Mansfield made his first appearance since early morning at the dinner-table. He and his brother-in-law were inordinately proud of their success for the day, as represented by several brace of dead birds. Thus restored to good humour with the world, Tom was never more genial than when raising one glass after another of Christmas cheer, till Fanny felt the room begin to swim about her. She was relieved when the interminable courses stopped, and the ladies could retire to drink tea and listen to a choir come from the village with a repertory of Christmas songs. These departed presently (replete with Christmas pudding and a silver guinea for their pains) shortly after the entrance of the gentlemen, when the task of entertaining the company was taken over by Mary on the harp and Julia at the piano.

Edmund and Jane had been allowed downstairs to join the adults during tea, and Fanny noticed with some amusement how her son secreted a slice of cake in his pocket – doubtless for the waiting Maria upstairs. His other pocket moved at the same time, revealing the hidden presence of Timmy. Fanny frowned, but decided not to make an open issue of it, but rather to send him out of the room as soon as possible.

She had reason to regret this decision almost at once, when Pug – always undisputed master of the drawing-room – sniffed out the presence of this low-born alien, who emerged to engage in an invigorating chase around the furniture to the gasps of the company, before stopping to defend himself energetically with arched back and bristling fur.

It was a skirmish in miniature, for Pug was a small dog, and his opponent was less than half his size, though compensating in courage, dexterity and ferocity for what he lacked in weight. While Pug growled, snarled and snapped, Timmy did battle in a whirlwind of slashing claws, spitting and leaping from chair to curtain in an astonishing display of agility.

The exchange was brief, the issue never really in doubt. Pug's barking changed to a howl, and he retreated under his mistresses' sofa to lick his wounds, while Fanny, who had seized the pop-eyed snarling victor, handed him over to his master before dismissing the pair of them to bed, *instantly*!

There being scarcely an inmate of Mansfield who had not felt the edge of his teeth about their ankles at some time, Pug's defeat was on the whole well-received, and Edmund's departure with the still bristling Timmy took on something of a triumphal air. Baddeley's grim smile and the footman's answering smirk went unnoticed, while the whole party canvassed the relative merits of feline versus canine. Humanity itself being divided on the basis of this universal topic, opinions were about as equally divided; and since everyone felt qualified to deliver their opinion simultaneously, it was an animated though somewhat incoherent debate.

The canine faction was predictably composed of Lady Bertram, Tom and Yates, reinforced by the elder Hunstons. These gave it as their opinion that the dog, in addition to being man's faithful companion, was also his stoutest defender – this position being somewhat weakened by the fact that Pug still lurked pantingly under his sofa.

Julia, morally supported by her daughter, was alone in declaring that the presence of any animal was intolerable in a civilised household. In view of her further acid comment on the 'Mansfield menagerie' it was as well that she was not living at the house two months later when William's present for his nephew arrived from Gibraltar – but that is to anticipate.

The feline defenders were less voluble, but nonetheless sincere. Mary, Stephen, Susan and Robert rather lamely – in view of Timmy's recent performance – vaunted the elegance, beauty and breeding of cats in general. Though Fanny's sympathies on the whole lay with this group, she had nothing to say, between annoyance at her son and the fact that in lifting Timmy he had sunk his claws into her forearm and delivered a deep scratch.

Henry gave it as his opinion that some individual animals were agreeable and some were not, irrespective of species, and then turned to where Fanny stood. Taking her arm, he drew back the sleeve to expose the red tear in the flesh, before dropping it and turning to ring the bell for the housekeeper. He said nothing but 'You had best let Manners take care of that,' before walking across the room to where Mary still sat at her harp, to solicit for another song.

Fanny turned to leave the room, ostensibly in search of the housekeeper, but in reality needing a few moments to recover her thoughts. It was not so much the importance of his action in itself, the calm yet rapid, almost impersonal manner in which he had held her arm, that was affecting her breathing. It was something else revealed by his gesture: an awareness of her presence and a sensitivity to her well-being that poor Fanny had not often encountered at Mansfield. It was what had drawn her initially to Edmund, and what she had learned to do without in his absence. In this house, everything was calm and mannerly, but it was not often that one sensed a warm interest in one's welfare, or felt valued for one's personal worth.

When she came downstairs twenty minutes later, two other subjects were under discussion. The first one concerned the next morning's service, which the whole house was expected to attend, it being Christmas Day. Since there were two services, nearly everyone elected to sleep late and attend the later one, though Fanny privately decided to wake in time to go to the earlier one on her own, if the weather allowed it.

The second subject was the means of conveyance for the following evening – the Mansfield ball was bearing early fruit, and the entire company was invited to an informal supper, followed by dancing, at the Olivers', three miles off. In this instance, the object was to try and make do with two vehicles instead of three. Henry insisted that he would go alone in his curricle, weather permitting, and Mary thought that she would wait and see how she felt to-morrow evening, while Lady Bertram awoke for long enough to announce that she did not think that she would be equal to such an enterprise. Fanny was surprised that this had even been considered, and made another private decision to offer to stay and spend the evening quietly with her aunt. The ball of the night before having left many with a deficit of sleep, it was unanimously decided to turn in early.

And now, as we dismiss our heroine to the conventional sleepless night, the discerning reader will have already deduced from the number of remaining pages that events are moving towards a conclusion of some sort. The general tone of the work will suggest that this is an appropriately happy one; but, in fiction as in life, the tragic denouement can never be ruled out. The reader by this time can scarcely be in a greater state of suspense than our heroine, who – it is obvious by now – is not only unsure of the gentleman's intentions but equally so of her own wishes in the matter. As we have already pointed out, Fanny was in some respects unsatisfactory material for a heroine; and this is best illustrated by the fact that she had as yet no clear idea of what she wanted or expected from Henry Crawford. Unheroic as this state of mind may be, it is probably more common than great works of literature may lead us to suppose. A heroine may be elected for the distinction precisely because of the clarity and incisiveness of her mind, but this does not apply to the rest of us, who often go dithering through life on a basis of haphazard decisions that are unrelated to any grand design.

In support of our heroine it must be pointed out, that in despite of his growing attraction for her, she had some cause to doubt the purposes of Henry Crawford in general, and as yet she had no certain knowledge of his serious intentions with regard to herself. This situation we intend to remedy in the course of the following day, and after that to leave Fanny to her own devices, whether heroic or otherwise.

21

*O*n Christmas morning Fanny arose from her restless couch early, whence an inspection of the world outside her window served to lighten her spirits. Though the ground bore some traces of a light snowfall, there was a cold clear sky, with more than a promise of blue for later in the morning. Thus provided with ideal weather for walking, an hour later she was to be seen briskly approaching the little church, awakened and refreshed by the invigorating walk.

The first person she saw on entering the dim doorway was Dr Thwaite. Somewhat to her surprise, he did not approach her smilingly as was his Sunday custom – instead his face crimsoned over, and with barely a 'Good morning', he turned and walked rapidly away to the vestry, where he was awaited, for Fanny was slightly late, and the bell had stopped ringing several minutes ago. The congregation was sparse at this first service of the day, but as Fanny passed rapidly down the aisle a few nods and smiles were in order in each direction, so that she entered the family-stall, seated herself and opened her hymn-book before noticing the only other occupant – whose colour almost rivalled that of the parson's on meeting her eye.

Fanny had chosen the early service from a need to recollect her thoughts in prayer in the privacy of a half-empty church, without the crowded distraction of the later service, which would be attended by almost the entire household at Mansfield. She had not thought to start Christmas Day by assisting at divine service in the sole company of Henry Crawford, seated in the dim seclusion of the family stall, her mind in a state of confusion and unable to concentrate on the words of the celebrant.

136

She got through the service by dint of keeping her head reverently bowed and avoiding any glance to left or right, but her difficulties were not finished after it was over. She had waited behind, hoping that Henry would be gone before she walked outside, but as she neared the open doorway she could see where he stood waiting, obviously for her. To compound her embarrassment, the parson broke from a conversation with two old ladies and approached her, smiling genially with hand outstretched, obviously determined to say something he had been unable to say earlier.

'Ah, Mrs Bertram! My very best wishes for the season – I hope you were pleased with our simple celebration?' Not waiting for a reply he continued in a lower tone, speaking quickly: 'Normally I would have great pleasure in a private interview with you sometime this morning, but you will understand that my duties today make that impossible. Since I am invited to luncheon at Mansfield, may I hope for a few words with you then?'

His face was reddening again, and he seemed to be trying to catch her eye as he spoke. A wild thought darted into Fanny's mind, relating to the letter from the Parsonage, which lay unopened on her writing-table. Feeling it expedient to do no more than nod and smile, she moved away rapidly, her mind still so full of this odd notion that she gave Henry a smile and the season's greetings, and set out for the walk home without any excessive degree of self-consciousness.

They walked on in the crisp air, the white silence broken only by the bells behind them. After a few moments, Henry opened a conversation with: 'I cannot think what impulse brought me here this morning. Were you surprised to see me?'

She was unaware that church attendance had formed any part of his previous life, and could not help saying so.

There was a slight grimace of the mouth as he replied: 'You are right. I was never brought up to it, and church-going has not been my practice for several years now. Before I left England, I had so much I wanted to escape from – so much guilt and misery – that flight, senseless activity and pleasure became ends in themselves.'

She interrupted him eagerly: 'But it was not always so! You were used to think and talk seriously, at one time – ' She broke off, too embarrassed to continue.

After a pause of some seconds he replied: 'Yes, that was here at Mansfield. I was very much in love at the time, and had some hopes for a future full of happiness.'

A long silence fell after these words, which seemed to reverberate on the cold air. She bent her head, closing her eyes as though to seal them inside her. As they walked, she had the impression of becoming progressively less conscious of her surroundings, till she reached the stage of not knowing in which direction they moved.

At last he turned towards her once more, and she noticed that his eyes bore the strained look caused by sleeplessness. 'How is your arm this morning?'

Although it had burned and throbbed in the night, she smiled and nodded silently. After another glance at her he continued: 'Are you cold? Will you take my greatcoat? I did not think to bring the curricle out so early.'

She shook her head, for they were nearly home, the bells behind them growing less deafening every minute, and the lodge gates just visible through the trees. Crossing the park, she withdrew her hand gently from his arm, and they reached the back door of the house in silence. Inside the still-sleeping house, she went quickly upstairs to her room, needing time for introspection. But had she not just come from church? Yet she felt more in need of guidance than when she left the house this morning.

On entering her room, her eye fell immediately on the letter that had come from the Parsonage the previous evening, and she opened it at once.

It confirmed her worst apprehensions. Through some of his influential connections, the incumbent of Mansfield had received an offer: the rectorate of a fashionable parish in London. He would be quitting Mansfield quite early in the coming year – but did not want to leave, nor even to publish his success abroad, without assuring Mrs Bertram of his warmest admiration. He went even further to promise her that if she placed her future in his hands, he would do his best to ensure their mutual happiness, as well as that of her son. This task would be rendered easier by the improved circumstances guaranteed by his new position, though as she was doubtless aware, he had private means, sufficient to overlook her own lack of any adequate provision. He looked forward to a meeting with her at her earliest possible convenience, to further discuss this important matter. He remained her devoted etc.

During her walk home from church, Fanny had forgotten the sudden thought that had occurred to her when confronted by the parson's bashfulness and manifest determination for a private meeting with her. She now had to sit down and think of a way of dealing with this newest problem – though there was no question in her mind that the doctor must be refused, the fashion of his refusal and his reaction to it might carry repercussions for Susan and Stephen.

For the second time in her life, Fanny found herself facing the refusal of an uncommonly advantageous offer of marriage out of hand, without considering the benefits it might have for the rest of her family. As in the case of the first proposal, received many years ago, she was certain that most of the inhabitants of Mansfield and the neighbourhood in general would cry out at her good fortune, and declare her refusal incomprehensible.

Here was a good man prepared to take a relatively portionless widow with a child (though it was true that the child was well provided for on his majority, no one had troubled with a formal settlement at the time of Fanny's marriage, though Sir Thomas had always intended to rectify this omission), and guarantee them a future existence of comfort and security; and the widow would not even contemplate the offer seriously – for what reason? Unwilling to pursue her thoughts any further, Fanny broke them off, and went downstairs to breakfast.

She considered penning a reply to Dr Thwaite which might release her from the need of an interview with him, but on reflection she decided that he deserved somewhat better treatment, even at some cost to herself. His intentions were honourable, his offer correctly made, and it was not his fault if her mind was preoccupied with someone else, who did not necessarily have any notion of marriage.

What if the proposal had come from Henry Crawford? The suggestion shot through her suddenly, so that she missed a step, and had to keep herself from stumbling across the doorway of the breakfast-parlour. She had to admit to herself that if such were ever the case, it would merit serious consideration, but she could not find any answer within herself, not as yet.

Surprisingly, the only person at breakfast was Mary, who said she was very hungry, and declared her intention of retiring for the afternoon after the service – Fanny and Julia would need to do the honours with the guests at luncheon. Edmund entered next, and after greeting his parent gravitated directly to Mary's side. The attraction that Mary held for her son never failed to mystify Fanny, for her cousin's wife, though occasionally kind after her fashion, never attempted to communicate directly with the little boy. It was rather as though her very indifference was interesting to him, and he hung with delight on her careless speech, on the way she dropped items of interest and anecdotes of personal experience. Fanny remembered how his father's initial reaction to Mary had been similar, and she was able to smile. These days Edmund left Mary's side directly if he caught sight of Henry, but neither brother nor sister could hold ground against the fascination of Ahmed. If her son continued to meet Ahmed 'by accident' at the stables in the afternoons, Stephen himself would soon be supplanted.

In this situation the balance was held by Maria, who though she was Timmy's slave and Edmund's handmaid, had something of her mother's strong will, and would often insist on a particular game or scheme when Edmund had other plans. As it is not interesting to be a follower without in turn being followed, Edmund dimly appreciated the importance of Maria for his own self-respect, and on this ground tolerated some of her more imperious commands. Soon after breakfast Fanny watched them set out for the woods, on an expedition organised by Maria, accompanied by Jem, to search for holly and mistletoe to decorate the hallway for the guests that were expected at luncheon. Jane made a protesting and tardy camp-follower, lagging behind the others and carrying the basket.

Later in the morning Fanny spent some time sitting quietly with her aunt, Mrs Hunston and Susan, completing and wrapping the small items of needlework that would be presented, with gifts of money, to the estate-workers during an evening reception the next day. Julia had been invited to join them, but had indignantly protested against spending an hour of Christmas Day taking care of shirts and handkerchiefs for the estate-workers when she had so much to do for her own children – who were not to be found anywhere – Mary was obviously the most proper person for such a task. Julia's speech was interrupted by the entrance of Edmund and his cousins, somewhat the worse for wear from brambles, but carrying a sufficient quantity of leaves and berries for a bouquet. Julia's ire was roused as much by the condition of her offspring's clothes as at the fact that they had departed illicitly from the house, and her mood was not improved when Jane insisted that it was all Edmund's fault, being abetted by Maria. Watching Edmund and Maria defending themselves stoutly, obviously in league with each other, Fanny felt more amusement than irritation, even when Maria was dragged bawling upstairs, with the terrible threat of not being allowed downstairs for tea, at which the children were to get their 'surprises'.

Luncheon proved to be a quiet affair: the dozen or so guests arrived in that seasonal mood of good cheer that makes entertaining very simple. At one point she heard Susan ask Tom the whereabouts of Henry and Stephen, and found herself listening for the reply: they had gone out to – he rather thought it was Ashfield, but could not be sure – after breakfast. Tom imagined it was something to do with the Christmas presents for the children that had been collecting for weeks, and were due for distribution today. It was to be hoped that he had not gone too far, as the good weather of the morning had given way to strong gusts of icy wind with the promise of a heavy snowfall later that night.

The sight of Dr Thwaite's rotund form and beaming countenance cost her a pang, especially when at the moment of the guests' departure he approached her for the first time with: 'Mrs Bertram, may I have the honour of a few words with you in private?'

Thinking it best to get it over with as soon as possible, Fanny led him to the breakfast-parlour, where the absence of a fire might hopefully reduce the length of the interview. She signalled for him to be seated, and being seated herself, waited for him to begin.

Though anyone may consider oneself licensed to laugh at the follies and inconsistencies of mankind, it is no part of this work to poke fun at the inadequacies of such a worthy soul as Dr Thwaite. He will therefore be allowed to conduct his proposal in private, and the reader will not be told any details beyond the following: firstly, the good doctor had no suspicion that his suit could prove unsuccessful, and initially persisted in thinking that Fanny had not understood his demand. Secondly, he refused to believe that the lady of his choice could be so imprudent as to refuse such an unexceptionable offer, no matter what her personal sentiments.

Fanny was obliged to repeat herself in several different ways before her message penetrated his understanding, and even then she was uncertain that he had accepted it, until he asked her outright whether her affections were engaged elsewhere. At this, her hesitant blush was enough; he acknowledged defeat gracefully, wishing her every future happiness, which she heartily reciprocated, and they parted friends with a cordial handshake. The ease with which this was effectuated suggested that his regard had been largely imaginary, and the relief afforded by the successful conclusion of this conversation lasted for the rest of the afternoon. Just as she had been apprehending luncheon, Fanny found herself in expectation of tea.

On observing the presents that had been preparing for the children for several days, Fanny noticed that toys destined for boys and younger girls are usually designed on a principal of noise. Edmund and Maria had their fill of a pair of drums, a trumpet, a whistle, a miniature harp, a music-box and various squeaky dolls and animals. Even some relatively inoffensive lead soldiers could not be played with without hallooed alarms and excursions, and incessant cannonade. Jane's offerings differed: a needlework set, crochet needles and silks, a lace collar with several bows and sashes and a pair of silk stockings pleased her immensely, and confirmed her in silent superiority, in contrast with the noise that the other two were making with their toys. Henry arrived with Stephen in the middle of the din, laden with more objects destined to increase its volume and reinforce the conviction that everyone was having a good time.

The good things being eaten, and a fair proportion of the toys silenced or rendered inoperable, there was nothing for the children to do but to go to bed. The adults were thus liberated for their own pursuits, which in this case was simply to prepare for their evening engagement. Fanny had already decided to spend a restful evening with her aunt – Lady Bertram had borne up very well under the festivities so far, but she was beginning to look fagged, and her niece was convinced that an early night would do her good.

A discreet knock on Fanny's door announced a visit from Susan, calling to ask an opinion:

'Do you think this dress is too bright – I have never worn pink!'

'It is very becoming, with your dark hair, but how is it I have never seen it before? And the one you wore the other night, at the ball – '

Susan laughed happily. 'You must have been so confused! They were Betsey's dresses, presents from Fitzjohn – she swore she never wanted to see anything from him again. So you see, Fanny, I am profiting from the wages of sin.'

Fanny could not help smiling at her sister, so pretty and blooming as she appeared, and so confident in her love. Susan wanted to know whether she could take her sister's place for the evening:

'For Stephen understands perfectly, and has agreed to stay behind to keep me company with our aunt.'

Fanny was only slightly tempted, for as she explained to Susan, her arm was still burning and she felt mildly feverish, so that an early night would do as much to restore her as it would Lady Bertram. Half an hour later she heard the carriages leaving, as she left her room to go downstairs.

22

*I*f Fanny thought that a quiet evening spent in the company of her aunt would serve to restore her health she was right, for her arm ceased to throb quite soon, and as the hours passed she no longer felt feverish. If she had hoped for a similar restoration of her sanity, however, she was wrong; for after an hour of Lady Bertram's plaintive demands and melancholy suggestions she was asking herself why she had not taken up Susan's kind offer, and gone to where there was light, music and the possibility of stimulating conversation. Despite trying again and again to see the wisdom of her decision to remain at home, something inside her rebelled against it, and wanted at all costs to be in the Olivers' friendly house, three miles away, together with the others.

It was a very quiet evening, for Lady Bertram was too tired for much conversation, and Fanny did not realise how much the weight of her thoughts silenced her tongue. Immediately after helping her aunt to bed, she returned downstairs to sit beside the fire with a book. This she only idly glanced at, in the moments when she was not leaning backwards in her chair, eyes closed, wondering what was happening at the Olivers'. She felt the loss of the evening intensely. At one point she heard the clock ticking on the landing – the dancing would have started by now. What if, like some modern Cinderella, she could be magically transported there on the instant? She saw herself enter, dressed in Mary Bertram's gown, and she experienced the pleasure of seeing someone walking towards her with the determination of taking her into the dance, his eyes fixed upon her face.

She must have dozed off for a short while, for when she awoke the candles were almost burnt down, and the room returning to firelight and dim shadows. The sound of a shutting door some-where in the house, accompanied by a chill draught of air, gave her a moment's warning, and in the next instant the door swung open and Henry stood before her, flecks of snow on his greatcoat, and mud on his shoes. He looked very tired, and that was perhaps the reason for the unceremonious way he spoke:

'You never came – I trust you are not sick? How is your arm?' With a quick gesture of impatience he moved towards her and seized hold of the arm in question, peering down at it in the firelight. 'It feels very warm – are you sure you are not ill?'

She nodded, wordless. Was it her recent sleep – of which a half-dream was remembered – or something else that checked her tongue? They stood there staring at each other, with him holding her arm, for what seemed a long time. Suddenly he put it away from him almost violently and burst out:

'I cannot go on like this any longer. You must speak to me and tell me what to do. Shall – shall we ever be together ... shall we ever be married?' Without waiting for a reply he continued, speaking rapidly as though to himself: 'You must know by now that I still love you – my God, when did I ever stop?'

She trembled, and tried to speak, but in vain. How to speak when one does not know what to say? Her mouth opened and closed once, her eyes filled with tears, and suddenly she turned and almost ran out of the door, upstairs to her room.

But not to sleep. Twice in the course of the hour that followed, as she sat hunched in a chair at the foot of her bed before she put herself to sleep, she almost came downstairs looking for him. In each case she was stopped by the same problem: what did she have to say to him? We already know that Fanny was one of those people, probably rare among heroines, who need time to collect their thoughts and reach a conclusion, especially on momentous issues. She was just beginning to realise that she might be in love with Henry Crawford, but this feeling was very different from what she had ever felt for Edmund, and before she was sure of herself in this, she did not even want to consider the idea of marriage.

So she tossed and turned miserably, heavy with tiredness but unable to sleep till, just after the clock struck one, there came a soft knocking at her door. Thinking that Susan might want to talk about the evening, she invited the caller inside, and was surprised to see Mary Bertram, diamond earrings askew, her expression uncharacteristically concerned.

'Henry left early – did you see him?'

What answer could Fanny give, except a somewhat lame nod, and then await the next question?

Instead of asking another, Mary approached the bed and stood looking down at Fanny. Despite the dim candle-light, perhaps she noticed the drawn look and the unshed tears, for her voice sounded gentler: 'Fanny, there is something I must tell you – I think Henry is still in love with you.' Mary's eyes were careful, and for once her voice held no hint of laughter. 'Will you please – please be careful with him – he was very badly hurt ... that last time.'

Fanny did not pretend to misunderstand, but she had the same difficulty finding something to say to the sister as she had earlier with the brother.

Seeming not to notice her silence, Mary continued: 'If you do not want to marry him, tell him so outright, and I do not think that he will ever trouble you again.' She raised her hand to her forehead, as though in weariness, before adding: 'Why am I talking to you like this? It's just that I know how highly strung he seems to have become, since his return from India. He has never spoken to me, of course, but I know him well enough.'

Feeling all the awkwardness of continuing silence, Fanny mumbled something about 'not feeling ready as yet to think about marriage', at which Mary burst out: 'Marriage! Did you *ever* really have a marriage? You went straight from loving one sort of brother to another! Fanny, *when* are you really going to fall in love – I mean with some outside the family and Mansfield, someone *separate and dangerous?*'

Without noticing the look of shock on Fanny's face she went on: 'Will you at least promise me to be kind to him?'

The idea of Mary Bertram, cynical and ruthless as she was, begging her to be kind to the notorious Henry, could have operated one of two ways – and Fanny's response was to burst into tears. Mary reached out and patted her shoulder awkwardly, murmuring that of course she knew that Fanny was kindness itself and incapable of cruelty, but she was so afraid for her brother, who had never seemed so unhappy before, and now she was at peace herself she only wanted the same for him.

Fanny hardly heard any of this – she was wiping her eyes on the hem of the sheet when she felt Mary kiss the top of her head, and looked up at the closing door.

★★★

Early next morning a note lay under her door. She trembled on recognising the hand, but lost no time in opening it. This is what she read:

You had no words to answer me last night – I speak to you once more, for the last time. Fanny, these years of separation and loneliness have been enough. I have loved you for long, but find that I cannot continue living like this without any hope of happiness. I am sick of loneliness, and hungry for a home and family, and these I intend to have, if not with you then with someone, anyone who will have me. I do not need words from you. I shall take a walk on the South Terrace after luncheon today. If you join me, I shall know there is hope. Otherwise I shall leave Mansfield tomorrow.

H.

The writing was blurred and hurried, as though written in great haste, with some words written over, and others heavily underlined for emphasis. Was this the elegant Henry? Putting aside her tray, Fanny read and re-read the note like a sleepwalker, feeling the paper, tracing the words with a finger, carrying it to the window to see if she could read any further depth of meaning into it. She could not turn her sight nor her thoughts from it for an instant, even interrupting her hasty dressing with pauses to stop and gaze on it. Never had she received such a communication! At the moment, she needed to think about her life, but she could think of nothing but her letter, and what he had written.

Did he really mean what he said? There remained in her mind a minute suspicion that this was perhaps the language in which fashionable people flirted with each other – she knew that he was

147

very experienced, and she did not know the degree of her own innocence and its power over him.

The first time he had proposed marriage to her she had not taken him seriously, for had she not just spent the summer watching his flirtation with her cousins? What language had he used with the youthful Fanny? She could not remember clearly, but it did not seem as awkward and ill-expressed as this note, and she could remember that his bearing had been confident, and full of his habitual charm. What had changed him? Perhaps the years of exile in a harsh country. Last night he had said that he had never stopped loving her – could that be true? Could the need for a home and family so work in a man that it impelled him towards someone who had refused him in the past, and who had been an unwitting cause of so much pain?

It was becoming impossible to direct her thoughts logically. They rather crowded in upon her and battered at her, as though from all directions, moving in a circle around the central issue, which was: *how did she, Fanny, think of him now, at this moment?* This is what her mind found most difficult to seize upon. Time and again the urgings of desire fell back before the sterner aspect of her cautious self, and after some time she had to stop as from actual fatigue and allow her thoughts to take a different direction.

There was a secondary problem, which touched upon the theme of home and family, that seemed so important to him, in his message to her. Mansfield was the only home Fanny had ever known, and in it lived her true family. Could she take a decision that would remove her from it for ever, and affect the lives of so many? Her thoughts moved around the circle again and came back to the starting-point – yes, she could, provided she loved him enough, and could trust him with her future. Trust seemed central to the issue, and what she must think more about.

For some time now she had ceased to hold him responsible for the scandal with Maria, except in the general sense that everyone must accept responsibility for one's unreflecting actions, for the arrow shot o'er the house. But there was little doubt that his way of life in general had not been what she could easily accept – would he change, or would he expect her to tolerate his habits, which she did not even know of?

Fanny felt some fear, and some doubt, when she considered how little she knew him. He was right when he said it was difficult to really know anyone, and he was also right in insisting that it was wrong to judge someone on the behaviour of a green summer thirteen years ago, but what else did she have to go on?

There was his kindness – the lengths to which he was prepared to help and please her and her family. Pacing up and down her room, she remembered William's promotion, and more recently Betsey's return to her mother. She remembered the tact and delicacy he had displayed on both his visits to Portsmouth. Stopping to interrogate herself in the mirror, she asked herself whether this was not enough: she knew something of the goodness which was in his nature, could she live with the rest? Did she love him enough for this?

Everything seemed to coalesce into a need for trust – the act of loving had to be this: *admitting one's need, and giving oneself up fully to another.* At this point, she stopped, and kneeling down beside her bed, she buried her face in the covers, for her thoughts now seemed so precarious, and her newly discovered feelings so vulnerable, that they must be hidden even from the morning light. In this position, with her hands convulsively clasping the covers about her face, she at last admitted the truth to herself: she loved him, she wanted a future with him, she would seek him out on the South Terrace today.

The effort of thought involved was so great that it resulted in tears. For long moments she lay back exhausted, racked by spasms of weakness, but when this had passed she felt at peace for the first time in days, and was flooded by a feeling of inner strength that she knew would take her through the day. Moving slowly, in an almost dreamlike state, she restored her dishevelled appearance as best she could, and went to see how Edmund and his cousins went on with their breakfast.

If Fanny's reactions seem somewhat excessive, one should bear in mind that, in addition to her essentially unheroic mould, which has been brought to the reader's attention before now, her present circumstances were peculiar. Not only had she received two serious proposals of marriage within twenty-four hours, after four years of solitary widowhood, but the gentleman for whose sake she had refused the first proposal was the gentleman of the second; and at the same time none other than the suitor she had consistently refused thirteen years ago, in the teeth of her family and friends. If she needed some time to adjust to her change of sentiments with regard to him, who shall blame her for it?

For years afterwards Fanny tried to remember the events of that morning, without success, for her faculty of memory seemed to have become suspended until after luncheon. She could recall isolated moments; a meeting on the stairs with her sister, who noticed how happy she looked, and later her aunt asking her whether she had done something to her hair, 'for you look somehow different'. At breakfast her son made no comment on her appearance, but thought it a good moment to ask for sixpence, and though Mary said nothing Fanny knew she was under observation, both from her and from Julia, who remarked once more on Fanny's feverish look, at which Mary smiled consideringly.

In fact, the only thing she could remember doing that morning was visiting the village schoolmaster in his cottage beside the schoolroom, in the trap with Stephen. Fanny's income did not allow her the luxury of any large charitable action beyond the scope of her work-box, but three years ago she had adopted five of the little orphans at the school, and saw them in shoes, shirts and school books every Christmas season. One of them was sick, the schoolmaster said, from an excess of the sweetmeats that Stephen had brought the day before. At this, Stephen disclaimed – it had been the Major's idea to raid the pastry shop in the village on behalf of the entire school – all sixteen pupils had been summoned, fêted and sent home rejoicing. Fanny could not imagine how Henry had heard of the school, much less of the orphans, until Stephen's sheepish look indicated his probable source.

On the way home, Stephen discoursed at some length on the excellencies of Major Crawford's character. Unintended as this was either to soothe or disturb her, the little that she registered of it was very much to her taste, and if the overall effect was to raise her feet even further off the ground, that was not entirely Stephen's doing.

Years later, she remembered nothing of what happened at luncheon except that Henry had arrived late, and taken a seat beside Tom to talk local politics. She had the impression that he was avoiding her, whereas in her mind nothing lived except the need to communicate with him. She looked at the world outside the windows several times – last night's snow still lay unevenly on the ground, it was crisp and clear under a thin grey sky, fine weather for an outing. The meal was over, and she had taken the desperate decision of going straight up to Henry and issuing an invitation to walk, when the head of the house arose, cleared his throat and made an announcement. The French say that eating stimulates the appetite, and who knows whether this reasoning works as well with other activities – the fact remained that since the Mansfield ball, the master of the house was inclined for another session of the performing arts, and wished for his family and guests to participate.

'And now, Mary and I invite you all to move to the drawing-room, where we propose to spend an hour in singing and playing to entertain my mother, who is feeling rather better today.'

Lady Bertram blinked in surprise. Nobody looked very interested, but in the face of such a direct request there was nothing for it but to follow everyone else into the drawing-room, and wait for the earliest opportunity of taking a walk.

23

*T*here were two things about the next hour that surprised
Fanny, and the first was how memorable she found it. Just
as the morning after Christmas Day passed with scarcely an
impression saved for later recollection, the impromptu concert
after luncheon lived on in her mind; many years later she was later
able to detail the programme to her children, beginning with the
aunts Mary and Julia singing a duet accompanied on the harp, and
could even remember that it was Jonson's ode 'To Celia'. Then
Tom had sung Lovelace's poem 'To Lucasta on going to the Wars',
and Yates had his opportunity of ranting through 'Friends,
Romans, countrymen'. When Mrs Hunston had finished warbling
'Cherry Ripe', Edmund sprang up and offered to do some verses
from 'The Solitude of Alexander Selkirk', but though he debuted
in fine style – monarch of all he surveyed – this petered out
somewhat in the second verse, and despite massive prompting from
the audience he never got beyond the desolate shore of the fourth.
His friend Maria also needed extensive prompting for her lisped
song 'Begonedullcare – I – pritheebegonefrom mee', although her
sister Jane's 'Fair daffodils we weep to see' was faultlessly executed.

The second surprise for Fanny was how much she enjoyed it.
As happens so often in life, an action commenced with low expectations turns into something of a revelation, and long before Henry
started to read Shakespeare, even while Stephen and Robert were
singing a Christmas carol, Fanny had become absorbed in the proceedings, and was conscious of an uncommon degree of enjoyment.

John Yates had put aside the large volume of *The Complete
Works* that he had used to refresh his memory, and this was idly
taken up and looked at by Henry, who when his turn came bowed

to Lady Bertram and asked whether she had any favourite passage? She needed several moments of reflection and some prompting to come up with 'The Seven Ages of Man', so that Henry was able to replace the volume on the empty chair beside Fanny before he started to recite the passage.

Henry was one of those rare speakers who combine a fine voice with intelligence, taste and sensibility. Fanny could remember having heard him read before at Mansfield, and even in the days when she was prejudiced against him and found his courtship oppressive, she had been fascinated by his performance. Her feelings today were indescribably different, and the effect of his voice upon her correspondingly magnified. But she said little at the general applause that followed, during which he was universally solicited to continue reading further passages. Henry came over to where Fanny sat beside the fireplace, and taking up the volume started leafing through it rapidly:

'Shall we read something from one of the histories? Here is *Henry the Eighth*. No, no, I think not – (with a half glance at Fanny) I doubt whether the work is favoured in every quarter. What about *Troilus and Cressida*? "*Oh that I thought it could be in a woman –* " no, it will not do either. Or what think you of this: "*How now Malvolio?*" "*Sweet lady, ho, ho*" … maybe … Wait, here are the sonnets. One can always find a sonnet to speak to one –' and almost immediately he launched into,

'*Shall I compare thee to a summer's day?*' and when that was over, was immediately asked for,

> *Being your slave, what should I do but tend*
> *Upon the hours and times of your desire?*

There was complete silence while he read, even the children did not move. Fanny sat clasping her hands in her lap, exactly as she had done, before, in this very room. She made no pretence of doing anything else, but listened with her whole being, gradually raising her eyes and fixing them on his face, spellbound with the power of the poetry and the music of his voice.

He completed the sonnet he was reading before looking up from the page, directly at her. 'Shall I read the next one? Hmm … maybe not. I prefer the sound of this – ' and he started reading, '*No! Time, thou shalt not boast that I do change*'.

At the end of the poem, he approached Fanny, and bending directly over her and speaking fast and low, he presented her with the open page: 'Do you know this one? Shall I read it?'

Fanny saw the first line of the sonnet he had indicated, breathed deeply, and murmured 'Please do, it is one of my favourites', before shivering at her own daring as he started,

> *So are you to my thoughts, as food to life,*
> *Or as sweet season'd showers are to the ground,*
> *And for the peace of you I hold such strife*
> *As 'twixt a miser and his wealth is found:*

Here there was a break in the reading, for Henry was holding the heavy volume so clumsily that it slipped from his fingers and fell to the hearth. He bent to retrieve it and quickly re-found the passage, but either from the effort of stooping in such proximity to the fire or from some other reason, he was very red and somewhat short of breath when he straightened and started to read once more. He completed the reading in a voice which gasped, hesitated, and more than once stumbled over the words, to the puzzlement of a few of his auditors. The last line he read slowly, and then closed the book decisively and laid it aside.

'Our revels now are ended with a vengeance. I am in need of exercise and some conversation, and propose to take a short walk on the South Terrace.' Here he looked down directly at Fanny and continued speaking: 'Mrs Bertram, would you care to accompany me? We shall certainly be back before dark.'

Edmund started to say something but was immediately silenced by Susan. Fanny arose quickly without speaking, and they walked out of the room to the hall for their cloaks. Immediately afterwards the door of the house closed behind them.

★★★

Some minutes later they could be seen strolling towards the gates of the park. She had taken his arm, and her left hand, which was inside her muff, was closely clasped with his right one. If such a method of locomotion served to reduce their pace, this did not

154

seem to be a problem, for the fact that they gazed at each other far more often than they looked down at the ground meant that any faster rate of walking was probably unwise. At first they had walked along the South Terrace, and then by mutual consent moved on to the flagged walk that circled the white and silent garden till they found the path leading to the gates. They had not yet exchanged many words, but everyone knows that these are one of the least favoured forms of communication between lovers.

Nevertheless, in some circumstances, they are the only means to hand, and after a lengthy interval of merely looking at each other, smiling and each gently breathing the other's name as though hearing it for he first time, speech at last seemed necessary.

Henry began by asking: 'Do you know where we are going? Not that it matters in the least ... '

Fanny smiled. 'I am taking you to my tree in the woods, where I often go in the afternoons. I thought I had mentioned it, the other day?'

'No, but so intensely curious am I about the way you spend your time that I could never do with questioning and teasing you. How did you receive my note?'

'Like a thunderbolt. But in fact, your sister had paid me a visit late last night.'

'Did she mention me?'

'That was the aim of her visit, to tell me that she – that she thought you still – loved me, and to ask me to be kind to you.'

She had thought he would laugh, but instead he stopped and stood facing her, taking both her hands in his. 'Will you promise me never to allow any member of our families to come between us? Mary means well, but is accustomed to interfering. Has she been writing to you about me?'

'Yes.' They walked on, and there was a silence of several minutes before Fanny continued, hesitantly: 'She mentioned your projected marriage and speculated on why it broke off. And she also mentioned a – a mistress ... a native one.'

They had reached her fallen tree and seated themselves, though not very comfortably, before Henry spoke again, still clasping one of her hands in both of his:

155

'Though I cannot deny that my past has been littered with such relationships, there was no native mistress. She was my legal wife for over seven years, and if we had had children, we might still be married. I will tell you all about that some other time.' Obviously, he would say no more on this subject at the moment.

'And the other ... ?' Fanny felt almost ashamed to ask, but the need for some sort of clarification was strong.

'I met Lisa Seton soon after my separation from Aziza. She was that rarest commodity in India – an unmarried Englishwoman. She was moreover young, pretty, from a good family and bent on marriage to a wealthy man, and her advent was hailed gratefully in our little circle. By this time marriage – or should I rather say, escape from loneliness – was my own single object, and for the three months of our total acquaintance, we were engaged for *two*. A fortnight before our wedding-day I received a letter, five months old, from Mary. She had just been to Everingham, and had news of Mansfield.'

'It was only *then* ... ?'

'Yes, that was the first I heard of your widowhood, and the fact that you had lived alone at Mansfield for four years.' Henry stopped for a moment before he continued speaking: 'Needless to say, Miss Lisa received her marching orders the next day, I had resigned my commission within the week, and was on my way to Calcutta before the month was out.'

'What did you tell her?'

'The truth. The woman I had always loved was widowed, and I wanted to return to England immediately. Fortunately there had never been a pretence of anything between us other than mutual convenience, and she was quite willing to release me, at a price.'

Fanny felt the unspoken embarrassment and humiliation behind his words, though these were lightly enough spoken. She went on to change the subject, 'Why did you leave Italy so soon? Mary had assured us that you were not expected at Everingham for another fortnight, at the earliest.'

'Why do you think?' He looked at her intently for several seconds before continuing 'I was sick of waiting and wanted an end to suspense. One afternoon in Florence, when I fancied I had seen your face in some frescoes in San Marco, I suddenly decided to cut short my stay in Italy and take the shortest way home.'

'Were you planning to meet me, on your return?' asked Fanny in wonderment.

'I had no other aim, and no definite plan except for a desperate idea of soliciting Mary's help in contacting you, and trying for a meeting, or even writing to you directly! If we had not met the day after my arrival at Everingham, I would have attempted any sort of communication with Mansfield, though there was some awkwardness at the thought of doing so.' He looked directly at her once more, and behind the smiling eyes she sensed rather than saw something of a past apprehension: 'You can imagine my feelings on learning that Mary was now mistress of the place, and was to visit me the very next day, in the company of just the person I had come all this way to meet.'

Before she could continue on this subject, Fanny needed a pause of several minutes to consider this information, and recall the shock of their meeting at Everingham. But first there was something else that required to be said: 'You need never feel awkward about Mansfield. The people living here know that many of them have cause to feel awkward about *you*.'

Henry struck his forehead with his fist in a mock tragic pose. 'I can see that my dear sister has been very busy on my behalf!'

Something else occurred to her: 'Did you not know of Mary's marriage before you left India?'

Henry shrugged. 'She wrote to me from Italy in August. The letter went to Delhi, and has not yet returned.'

There was a comfortable silence while he played with the fingers of the hand that he still held. Then, turning to look directly at her, he asked:

'What made you change your mind – I mean about me?'

Fanny hesitated. 'I really cannot tell. Ever since our visit to Everingham you have never been long absent from my thoughts, and even before your extraordinary act of kindness to Betsey, I had occasion to reflect on the way in which someone may live up to his reputation. Also how little one may really know a seemingly familiar person.'

Henry smiled. 'The ball? I have waltzed at least twenty times in my life, but the other night I trembled with nervousness. If you

157

only knew how often I had dreamed of waltzing with you!'

Fanny blushed. 'You cannot have been as nervous as I was – do not forget that I had to concentrate on my steps as well!'

'And then you looked so beautiful, I could not take my eyes from you during the concert.'

Fanny's only response to this was to colour more deeply.

Henry was ready with another question: 'Were you really so surprised to see me at Everingham? Did you not suspect?'

'I nearly fainted from the shock! It was the very thing I had secretly feared, and the last thing I really expected. Throughout supper I was asking myself why I had allowed myself to be persuaded to accompany them. I was terrified that you might think I was pursuing you – '

Henry laughed outright, and at length. 'That would be the very last thought to cross my mind! You looked absolutely aghast when you raised your head and saw me at the top of the steps, and the way you shrank from me at dinner, and again the next morning – I almost despaired!'

Fanny looked up eagerly. 'Yet the next morning, after breakfast, you never returned – '

Henry smiled again, slowly. 'You noticed that? You were meant to, but I was not sure you would. I certainly had important business elsewhere on the estate, but it would have waited for later had I not been convinced that your reluctance even to converse with me meant that no useful purpose would be served by seeing you again that morning. I know your nature, Fanny, and how you need time to accustom yourself to new ideas and situations. As serious as my intentions had become, I knew that everything could be spoiled by haste. Connected as we now were, I counted on the operation of time in my favour. Do not forget, that very morning I had received an invitation to spend Christmas at Mansfield!'

'And after that, what did you plan to do?'

'I had a scheme of getting Mary to invite you to spend some months with her in London.'

It was Fanny's turn to laugh. 'Mary might enjoy interfering in the affairs of her relations, but I doubt she would appreciate being made use of in that way!'

Henry was looking at her fixedly. 'Why am I so surprised at how beautiful you are when you laugh? Considering that I intend to devote a substantial portion of my life in future to the pleasure of watching you smile, you must do it more often.'

'On the contrary, I have done nothing but smile and blush since the evening of the ball – and Julia, for one, nurses some strong suspicions about us.'

'Let her! She will soon have confirmation of every one of them.'

They could have talked for hours, perched in discomfort on the tree-trunk, with the rotting scraps of diary littered about them in the dead leaves and snow under their feet – but shadows were beginning to lengthen, and they were awaited at the house. Though they could rejoice in the prospect of a lifetime of conversation that lay ahead of them, in the meanwhile there was barely time enough on the walk home to talk of an eventual wedding. For Henry, it could not be too soon, or informal enough. He had already procured a special licence ('*Why do you think we were late leaving London, and where do you think I went yesterday?*') and if she was agreeable, he was prepared to drive off with her the very next morning. Resisting the temptation to ask him whether he made a common practice of elopement, she found it harder to disguise the fact that she was at first mildly shocked and then titillated at the idea that he had planned their marriage so early, even before he had in any way assured himself of her consent. Here was matter for hours of gentle teasing, but in the meanwhile they could decide on at least one thing. She agreed with him on the need for a wedding that was both small and private, but earnestly requested that it take place at Mansfield, probably just before Tom and Mary departed for London. That would be within the next few weeks, and had to satisfy Henry, who shrugged at the idea of so many Bertrams at his wedding.

'What else should I expect, in marrying a Bertram? We will go to Everingham directly, and from there – where you will. Do you want a wedding trip to Greece, or would you prefer Italy?'

They had not yet decided on this when they reached the house and went upstairs to prepare for dinner, but they had agreed to try and keep their secret for another day or two, if that were possible.

24

*T*his resolution was easier to make than to keep. Starting with the very next gathering that same evening, she could see that they were being watched not only by certain family members, but by some of the staff, and even by a few tenants of the estate, gathered at Mansfield for the purposes of conviviality and largesse. Though careful not to betray the situation by any undue word or look, she could deduce not only from Mary's smile and Yates' handshake, but more significantly perhaps from Baddeley's bow, that it was optimistic to think of concealing the truth from anyone for more than another day at the utmost.

Mary approached her that evening after dinner under the pretence of bringing her another cup of tea, and turning her back upon Baddeley where he was busy with his urn, she lowered her voice confidentially: 'I do not agree with my dear sister Julia that you look ill today. *Au contraire*, I find that you have been looking extremely well recently, and today better than ever. Is there any reason for this impression?' She then laughed heartily at Fanny's confused response, patting her knee and smiling. 'You are quite safe from me, you know – even Tom shall wait to hear it from the horse's mouth,' before moving to where her husband stood chatting to his estate-manager.

Fanny had decided to speak to her sister that very night, and followed her upstairs to her room to make the important communication. Though half-expectant, Susan's joy was so spontaneous and so infectious, that Fanny at last began to feel her own more strongly, as distinct from merely knowing it – and the sisters spent almost two hours in absorbing conversation. Susan immediately felt all the advantages of the match, not merely for the happy pair, but for both their families, and was, if possible, even more optimistic than Fanny herself for the chances of their future happiness, which she rated as highly as her own.

Waking from her first good night's sleep in several days, the next morning she felt ready to take on the world, even though her first encounter was only with her son, who she wanted to be the next to know the news. Being pried away from Maria and a game they were in the process of inventing, he was not in the best of moods to hear her news; and after a preamble in which she demanded confidentiality, she found him only moderately interested in the changing perspective of his life. His chief preoccupations were firstly to ensure that Timmy could accompany them to Everingham, and secondly to ascertain that Ahmed would be a member of the household there. Thirdly, he inquired whether Susan, Stephen and Maria would have unlimited right of access to Everingham, and whether he could occasionally visit his grandmother and Jem at Mansfield. These bases secured, he gave the impression that it was relatively unimportant to him as to who exactly she married — certainly he admired Henry, but it was more for the quality of his horses and the services of the peerless Ahmed than for any other reason. Fanny sighed as she left him and went in search of Henry, hoping that it would not be long before the two men in her life arrived at a more just appreciation of each other.

She found him in the library, obviously waiting for her. The first manifestations of pleasure at their meeting over, Henry had something to say. He saw no reason to continue what was fast becoming an open secret, but was keen to publish his successful love to the world. Though she saw his point, Fanny begged for another day to give herself time to write to William and her mother, and to speak to her aunt on the critical subject. Lady Bertram could in one sense be considered as the ideal *belle mère* – so indolent and retiring as to be practically incapable of assuming an affront in most circumstances of daily life. In this precise conjuncture, however, even she might be expected to voice some complaint if she was the last to hear the news, or had the indignity of hearing of it from one of the servants. Fanny thought it would be wise to speak to her in the course of the day, and make the announcement at dinner that evening.

She then smilingly informed him of her son's reception of the news, to which his only comment was: 'He would probably have preferred for you to marry Ahmed!'

Fanny grew suddenly thoughtful. 'Will you miss your life in India? Are you sorry that you left?'

'Naturally there are some things that I miss, though on the whole, I am glad to be home again. I have few ties of sentiment to the place – no, wait Fanny', taking her hand and seating himself beside her while he looked at her with some concern, 'don't take what I say amiss. Are you thinking about Aziza?'

Taking her bent head and her silence for assent, he continued talking, slowly and carefully:

'She came from a respectable but poor family, her father was my Persian tutor in my second year of service, which is how we met. We made no pretence of a romantic attachment; our marriage was a practical arrangement (one that is very common out there, for most of our people live alone for years on end), which she entered into for the sake of financial security.'

He stopped, in case she wanted to speak, but she merely asked: 'You said you were legally married?'

'We went through a ceremony that was legal according to Indian law, but not binding outside it, and which allowed for a simple divorce provided it was mutual, especially in the eventual absence of children after some years together.'

'Why did you decide to divorce?'

'Her family moved to Agra and she wished to accompany them, so a separation became inevitable. The marriage contract, which I chose to honour, provided for a lifetime pension for her and her parents.'

'*Chose* to honour?'

'Fanny, you cannot imagine the rules of life out there.' Henry stopped speaking and looked directly at her. 'My relationship with Aziza is one episode of my life that I can share quite simply with you. There were others, especially after – ' he hesitated, searching for words, 'that I would find it difficult to talk about, and that I feel ashamed to remember. But my life in Delhi was the simple life of a Company soldier, unattractive as it is in some respects, and neither of us need have any doubts relating to it.'

162

Fanny felt impatient to think of the hours she had lost in worry on this subject, and was now eager to talk about something else, but could not immediately conjure up another topic – happiness seemed to have dulled her wits. Henry really wanted nothing so much as to sit contemplating her in the beatitude of their mutual feeling for each other, but there was something that he had long wanted to ask her:

'Tell me something, Fanny – when you married Edmund, all those years ago, did you love him?'

Fanny took time to answer, looking straight into his eyes. 'I thought I did. It seems I did not know the meaning of the sentiment at the time. Since then … '

Henry smiled. This information seemed to have settled some doubt in his mind, and he reached out to press her fingers gently before saying: 'It is no wonder I got nowhere with you in six months – if you knew how beneficial that experience was for me!'

There was another prolonged silence in the library before Fanny remembered something she needed to mention: 'I intend to write to my mother this morning, as well as to William. Do you have any messages for them?'

'I shall enclose a brief message for your mother and Betsey in your letter, but will write my own letter to William. Do you think he will be here in time for the wedding?'

'I earnestly hope so.'

Fanny smiled at him as she spoke, which gave him the excuse to remark: 'Did you know that one of your front teeth is slightly crooked – what shall we do about that?'

Resting his chin on his hand, he sat gazing at her teasingly, his eyes returning repeatedly to her mouth till she almost choked with embarrassment. Rational conversation being thus rendered impossible, Fanny lapsed into a similar silence, and not another word was heard in the library till Stephen entered casually, looking for a book, and checked abruptly at the sight of the Major and Mrs Bertram, evidently enjoying an intimate tête-à-tête. It was impossible to do otherwise than inform him of the situation before Fanny departed to write her letters, and to meditate upon how best to present the news to Lady Bertram.

It was with some trepidation, later that morning, that she chose a moment to lay aside her correspondence, turn to her mother-in-law, and request a few minutes' conversation with her on an important personal subject.

Lady Bertram raised her head from her fringeing and looked sombrely on Fanny. 'Certainly, my dear. As a matter of fact there are two things I have been wanting to discuss with you for several days. The first one is about Susan and Stephen.'

Fanny looked at up at her aunt, for there was something unusual about the tone of her voice. 'I have decided to do a little something for them, and have requested my lawyer to release three thousand pounds from my personal funds which can immediately be settled on Susan. In addition, I have suggested to Tom to make the Mansfield living over to Stephen for the moment, since Dr Thwaite tells me he is leaving [here there was a shrewd glance at Fanny], until Edmund is of an age to decide whether he wishes to take orders or no. In any case, there is also Thornton Lacey reserved for him, unless Tom needs it for his own son.'

Fanny could not help an inward smile at the idea of Mary's son taking Orders, but was otherwise silent from surprise. She could not recall ever having heard her aunt speak in this decisive vein; and though she knew her to be generous by nature, she had never known her empowered to make decisions like this one, that could affect the lives of others. Susan and Stephen would be able to marry immediately, quite apart from what she herself might be able to do for them in the future. Fanny's eyes filled with gratitude, and she turned to her aunt to say something, but Lady Bertram had continued speaking:

'This brings me to the second important personal subject about which I have wanted to talk to you. It concerns your approaching nuptials, which I feel obliged to point out to you seem somewhat ill-advised.'

There followed a pause of several seconds.

'You may feel it not in the best of taste for me to comment at this point, but I feel that the opinion of an older woman, a friend who has had many years of living experience, would not come amiss at this point.'

Fanny experienced a sinking feeling: this situation was precisely what she had feared most. Though she could not really admit the superior quality of life-experience that kept one sitting on a sofa all day long, she decided to let this pass. She was awed by the rarity of the occurrence; in all her years at Mansfield she had never received any practical advice from her mother-in-law on any important subject, which was possibly a good reason for her sincere affection for the lady.

Lady Bertram continued: 'You are still young, Fanny, and have many years of happiness before you if you choose wisely. I cannot help but feel that precipitation is more of a danger in the choice of a marriage-partner than in almost any other choice that we make in our lives.'

Fanny had never heard her aunt speak in this vein before – she was not even aware that Lady Bertram possessed the reflective possibilities inherent in her last statement. She listened silently.

'I have your best interests at heart, Fanny, and truly think that this man is not right for you.'

25

*T*here followed an awkward silence. The only thing that Fanny could find to say was: 'On what exactly do you base your objections, dear aunt?'

'Unsuitability as to outlook and style of living. He is considerably older than you, and obviously very settled in his ways. The fact that he has never married indicates an indisposition to the state which may be difficult to overcome, as will all his ingrained habits of solitude and possibly of vice. He obviously loves the pleasures of the table, and we may imagine how closely those of the flesh are associated with these. I already suspect him of hypocrisy, though I cannot absolutely convict him of it. But his least endearing trait is his pomposity. What misery you will have, Fanny, to listen for hours to his boring proses and sermons!'

Fanny heard this resumé of her intended husband's character in gathering perplexity, and it was not until the penultimate sentence that light finally dawned. But before she could say anything to reassure Lady Bertram, the good woman continued:

'I have come to believe that some degree of compatibility is a necessary ingredient for a happy marriage. My own – ' here she distinctly hesitated, then went on resolutely, 'my own marriage illustrated some of the ill-effects of a too great disparity of age and taste. Sir Thomas was eighteen years my senior, but that was nothing compared to the difference in outlook – he was a very stern man.'

Fanny could remember how often she had shivered, as a child, at his approach and at the sound of his voice.

'I was a very pretty, very giddy young girl at the time of my marriage, Fanny, but all that was knocked out of me in the first three years, long before the girls were born. Small wonder that I retreated to the drawing-room and my sofa!'

Another brief silence. Once more Lady Bertram appeared to hesitate slightly before continuing: 'Edmund, though young, was something like his father in some ways. I do not mean that he was stern, for he was all goodness, but he was not buoyant or gay – even as a child he did not laugh often. I think that now you need a *happier* sort of man – someone who would play with your son, who would make you talk and laugh, who would bring the colour to your face in the way that I have seen it sometimes lately.'

Fanny was both amazed and mortified at the revelation of this woman's real depth. She reproached herself for never having taken the trouble to understand her, being content with shallow affection when there was so much here to love and admire. This was the second example for her, in the past two days, of the danger of labelling people according to 'type' – even those whom she thought she knew extremely well. It was also an indication of how easy it is for the individual to break away from such arbitrary and facile modes of classification. As she sat staring at her aunt, she could not refrain from bursting out with: 'But why have you never spoken to me in this way before?'

There was a sort of grim half-smile before Lady Bertram replied: 'Who cares to take advice on this subject? The young need to live their lives and make their own mistakes, and the simplest way for the old to retain the affections of the young is by keeping their own counsel. But your happiness is too important for me, my dear Fanny, to watch you making the mistake of choosing the wrong sort of man for husband.'

Dry-mouthed, Fanny chose her words carefully: 'What sort of a man would suit me, in your opinion, my aunt?' Her voice fell almost to a whisper. 'What do you think of ... Henry Crawford?'

Her aunt was not looking at her, but was gazing into the distance, at the white garden beyond the drawing-room draperies.

'*He* is the type of man, when I was young – ' her deep breath was something of a sigh – 'But Fanny, such men are often poor husbands, and we both know what his life has been.'

She turned her head suddenly and looked directly at Fanny: 'Has he spoken to you again? We knew that he wanted to marry you all those years ago, but is it possible that his feelings have lasted?'

Poor Fanny was by this time in such a state of acute embarrassment that she would almost have preferred to re-live her initial *éclaircissement* with Henry than to reveal his deepest feelings to her mother-in-law. But the revelation could not be postponed. Blushing, stammering and searching for words, she gave Lady Bertram to understand that this was indeed the case, that she now earnestly returned his sentiments, and that though her aunt was mistaken as to the identity of her suitor, she was correct in her premise of Fanny's engagement and imminent marriage.

A silence of some intensity followed. Fanny sat still, looking down. Suddenly she heard her aunt arise, cross over to the chair beside hers, seat herself, and place one arm about her, while her other hand clasped both those of Fanny, which were folded in her lap. They sat like this in silence for some minutes, till it was broken by the barking of Pug from the doorway, indicating the arrival of the housemaid with more wood for the fire. Then Lady Bertram stood up, returned to her sofa and her fringe, and presently asked Fanny in a calm voice whether she had completed her letters.

But Fanny was never again deceived by her aunt, and knew that their common understanding would in the future be better than it had ever been in the past.

Lady Bertram made no further comments on Fanny's proposed marriage when it was announced at dinner that evening, beyond murmuring to her later, when the ladies had retired: 'The emerald set I think, dear Fanny – yes, I think that would be best with your hair and eyes. You shall have the emerald set that Sir Thomas gave me on our third wedding-anniversary. It is hardly worn, and the stones are very fine.' Then she addressed herself to Pug, who was on her other side, sitting up and begging for macaroons.

Julia made very little pretence of pleasure either in her initial reception of the news, or in a short conversation she had presently with Fanny across the table. Cutting short the exuberant congratulations of her spouse, she had nothing more to say than: 'I'm sure I wish you very well – though the wedding sounds like a hasty affair. Couldn't you wait to have it in London?' She knew better than to voice any criticism on the subject to Mary – here it was a false smile and an oblique comment on the end of Henry's career as a bachelor – to which Mary only flashed a smile of such archness as rendered Julia too uncomfortable to continue with the subject.

When the men came in later, and Henry came to sit beside her, he found Fanny pensive and uncommunicative.

'I can see that I must exercise all my charm tonight, to get you to smile. Did you notice the look on Julia's face when I made the announcement? What, not even the slightest dimple? Your hands are icy cold – come with me, and sit nearer the fire. Wait, let me rub them, obviously we will need more fires at Everingham next Christmas.' Then, looking searchingly into her face, 'Are those tears behind your lashes ... Fanny, my sweet, who has been making you cry?'

Fanny gazed into his concerned face for a long moment before asking, softly, 'Will you expect me to do nothing all day, at Everingham, but sit on a sofa?'

He finished wiping her cheeks gently and concealed a kiss in the palm of the hand that he held before answering: 'You may of course do that if it will make you happy, Fanny, my dearest, *but rather than merely existing I think that I would prefer for you to live.*'

★★★

The next morning brought a letter from William. It was really more by way of a note, announcing his arrival at Mansfield:

'for the end of the week, God willing, if all goes well this end, and that old b— Heywood does not find some new excuse to scuttle our plans once again. It is in the wind that I may be stationed at Portsmouth until the end of the year at least, and possibly beyond; which should bring some joy to the whole family, but especially to my Jane and the children. These last are due to arrive sometime before the end of February, and you can imagine how impatient I am to see them. In the meantime, I look forward very eagerly to seeing my sisters again, and to hearing that all is well with you and Mansfield.'

Even in the midst of her happiness at predicting William's response to her news, and her satisfaction that he would be present at her marriage, Fanny was host to some less interesting sensations on remembering the delicate task ahead of her today, when she must request the parson to officiate at the ceremony. The idea raised some feeling of pity, till this was dissipated in the course of the afternoon when she learned that he had been boasting of his new appointment in several houses of the district, and proposed shaking the dust of Mansfield from his heels before the end of May.

By then Fanny and Henry would have returned from their wedding-tour, and would pay a short visit to Mansfield to assist at Susan's wedding and take up Edmund for the return to Everingham. This arrangement meant that they would be travelling abroad in the early springtime, which of all the seasons of the year was the one most attuned to Fanny's sensibilities, mingling as it did freshness and tenderness with latent power and promise. Sincerely as she regretted missing the first buds at Mansfield this year, when she considered her own burgeoning prospects for future happiness, she felt amply compensated for the sacrifice.